Professor P

and the

Jurassic Island

D1439869

About the author

I was born in London in 1957 and studied Theoretical Physics at Corpus Christi College, Cambridge. After leaving University I began my work as an inventor, designing electronic and computer systems.

I now live in the West Country with my wife, son and our cat. *Professor P and the Jurassic Island* is my second children's book.

About the illustrator

Professor P

and the

Jurassic Island

P. J. Davidson

Illustrated by

A. T. Royce

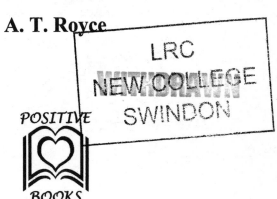

POSITIVE

BOOKS

Published by:

Positive Books Limited
66 High Street
Glastonbury
Somerset BA6 9DZ
Tel: 01458 832017
E-mail: info@ positive-books.co.uk
Website: www.positive-books.co.uk

First published in 2010

A CIP catalogue record of this book is available from
the British Library.

ISBN 978-0-9546151-1-6

Printed in the UK by CPI Cox and Wyman.

For my parents,

Daphne and Jake

Contents

Prologue

Dorset & Devon

Daily News

Friday, April 2

JURASSIC LANDSLIDE

The biggest landslide in over one hundred years occurred yesterday on the World Heritage Jurassic Coast in Dorset and East Devon.

Fossil hunters from all over the world are eager to discover what the landslide will reveal.

Local fossil expert, Dr John Simmons told our reporter. "This is an amazing chance to discover new fossils. I'm hoping we may uncover a giant sea reptile or possibly even a dinosaur!"

CHAPTER ONE

Fossil Find

"I wonder what we'll find, Peter!" Tara said excitedly as we raced down the hill towards the beach.

"I bet there'll be some great fossils!" I replied, panting.

When we reached the beach car park, I let Sparky, my golden Labrador, off the lead. He bounded down the steps and ran towards the sea, wagging his tail happily.

"Look at that!" Tara cried as we jumped down onto the beach.

I gasped in amazement. About two hundred metres away the cliff had collapsed, spilling mud and boulders all over the beach and out to sea. Huge grey rocks, the size of cars were strewn all over the sand!

A crowd of people were gathered by the landslide. Tara and I ran over to see what was happening. As we made our way through the crowd, I could hear everyone talking excitedly.

"It sounded like thunder!"

"It woke me in the night!"

"I thought it was an earthquake!"

"Lucky no one was hurt…"

We made our way to the front of the crowd and stopped at a rope strung up between two poles. On the other side of the rope, a camera crew was setting up.

"It's the BBC!" I exclaimed.

A short stocky man from the crew came over to the crowd and spoke to us in a loud voice.

"I'm the producer," he explained. "We're almost ready to start the interview, so please be as quiet as possible. Thank you."

Everyone quietened down. The producer went over to a woman with long dark hair and gave her a microphone.

"She must be the reporter," I whispered.

The woman brushed the hair away from her face and then began, "I'm here on the beach at Seatown in Dorset. With me is Dr John Simmons, a fossil expert from the Heritage Coast Centre in Charmouth."

Dr Simmons was a tall thin man with a serious expression. He looked slightly familiar.

"He came to our school last term," Tara said.

"Oh, yes," I replied, suddenly remembering where I had seen him before.

Dr Simmons had given a talk in assembly and shown us some of his fossil collection. We leaned over the rope and strained to hear what he was saying.

"Dr Simmons," the reporter continued, "Tell us about the landslide."

"Over five hundred metres of cliff have collapsed," he replied. "It's one of the biggest landslides we've had here on the Jurassic Coast and it will almost certainly have brought many new and interesting fossils out onto the beach."

"What kinds of fossils?" the reporter asked.

"Sea creatures mainly," he answered.

"Sea creatures?" the reported repeated, looking puzzled.

"These cliffs were laid down in the Jurassic period," Dr Simmons explained, "when the area was a warm, tropical sea, teeming with fish and squid. And preying on them were giant sea reptiles, the most common being the ichthyosaurus."

"What's an ichthyosaurus?" the reporter asked interestedly.

"It was a dolphin like creature with large eyes and crocodile teeth," he replied. "The first complete fossil of an ichthyosaurus was found here two hundred years ago by a girl called Mary Anning. She was only twelve years old when she dug it up."

"Only twelve!" the reporter exclaimed.

"Yes," Dr Simmons said, "and Mary Anning went on to make many other important discoveries here, including the first plesiosaur, a huge long necked sea reptile."

"And have any dinosaurs been found here?" the reporter continued.

"Dinosaur fossils have been found a few miles west, near Charmouth," Dr Simmons replied. "But they are very rare."

"Why is that?" the reporter asked.

"Dinosaurs lived on the land," he replied, "but occasionally was one swept out to sea and fossilised in the mud."

"Tara, we might find a dinosaur!" I said excitedly.

I felt a shiver of excitement run up my spine. This could be our chance to make a great discovery!

"Finally, what advice would you give to fossil hunters, Dr Simmons?" the reporter asked.

"Stay away from the cliffs," he replied firmly. "They are extremely unstable and dangerous. Another landslide could occur at any time, especially after all the heavy rain we've had during March. There's no need to go climbing on the cliffs as the best fossils can be found on the beach."

"Thank you, Dr Simmons," the reporter said with a smile. She turned back to face the camera and finished her piece.

When the interview was over, the crowd of people walked away. Sparky ran over to us and shook himself vigorously, sending water everywhere!

"Sparky!" I laughed. "You're soaking!"

"Woof!" he barked playfully.

"Come on, Peter," Tara said, tugging at my arm. "Let's go fossil hunting!"

We rushed over to a pile of freshly fallen rocks. I scanned the ground excitedly, wondering what I would find. I picked up a grey stone about the size of an apple and examined it closely. It had been buried in the cliffs for millions of years, and now it was about to reveal its secrets!

I placed the stone on a flat boulder and eagerly took my fossil hammer and goggles out of my rucksacks. I put on my goggles and raised the hammer. I held my breath in anticipation. Then I hit the rock hard. Crack! The stone broke in two.

"Anything, Peter?" Tara asked eagerly.

I picked up a piece of the stone and examined it. In the centre was a lovely spiral shell, milky white in colour.

"An ammonite," I replied, happily. "It's a good one too!"

The fossil shell shone in the sunlight. It looked so clean and new – it was difficult to believe it was millions of years old.

As I put the fossil in my rucksack, I heard Sparky barking madly. He was half way up the side of the cliff and chasing seagulls!

"Come down, Sparky," I called out sharply.

He looked at me and then turned to come down the cliff. I watched anxiously as he stepped over the loose stones, carefully trying to find his way down the steep slope.

Suddenly he slipped. My heart skipped a beat as he skidded, loosening a shower of rocks.

By the time Sparky regained his footing, an avalanche of rocks and boulders was tumbling down the side of the cliff.

Then, just above Sparky, a huge boulder broke loose!

"Sparky!" I cried in horror.

Sparky got out of the way of the boulder just in time. As the block fell it smashed into the side of the cliff, dislodging more rocks, which streamed down the cliff face.

Sparky scrambled down the slope onto the beach, only just avoiding the huge boulder as it tumbled after him.

"Look out, Tara!" I yelled.

The boulder bounced a few times and then smashed onto the beach a short distance away, sending a shower of pebbles into the air. I turned and shielded my face as the sharp stones flew everywhere.

"Are you all right?" Tara asked when the shower had stopped.

"I'm OK," I replied. "No harm done."

Sparky ran over and lay shaking at my feet. He was terrified. I sat down on the beach beside him and stroked him gently. I could feel his heart pounding from the shock.

Tara went over to the fallen boulder.

"Peter, come over here!" she called.

I stood up and went over to join her.

"Look at this!" she said, pointing to a dark marking on the boulder.

I bent down next to Tara and inspected the boulder. It had cracked along one side and a piece of rock had broken away to reveal a fossil. It was about a centimetre long and shaped like a triangle.

"It looks like ..." I began.

"A tooth," Tara interrupted. "It's a tooth!"

We dashed over to our rucksacks and grabbed our tools. I quickly put my chisel against the rock and raised the hammer.

"Careful, Peter!" Tara warned. "We don't want to damage it."

Tara was right. I lowered the hammer and tapped at the rock gently. Tara joined in and we loosened a section of rock above the fossil. We prised away the loose section and a large piece of rock fell to the ground with a crash.

I gasped in astonishment. We had uncovered three more teeth! I stared at the fossil in amazement. We had never found a fossil like this before. It was as good as one from a museum!

"Oh Peter," Tara cried excitedly. "I think we've found a dinosaur!"

CHAPTER TWO

Professor P

Tara and I knelt down and excitedly examined the fossil.

"I think this is part of the jaw bone," I said, tracing the outline with my hand.

"I bet there're lots more teeth buried in the rock," Tara said eagerly, "maybe even the whole head!"

"If we chisel just here," I said, pointing to a small crack in the boulder, "I think the rock will break away and we'll be able to get to the rest of it."

I put my chisel into the crack and raised the hammer.

"Wait, Peter!" Tara cried suddenly. "You might break it! It's not worth the risk!"

Tara was right. It would be so easy to damage the fossil with the thick chisel. We would need much better tools if we were going to get the fossil out safely.

"Let's ask Mary for help," Tara suggested. "She'll know what to do."

"Good idea," I agreed,

Mary was the owner of the Fossil Shop in the village. She had always helped us with our fossil collecting and we sold her our best finds. She also had the special drills and tools we would need to get the fossil out of the rock safely.

"I'll run to the shop and get her," Tara said, jumping up. "You wait here with Sparky and guard the fossil."

"OK," I replied.

Tara ran off and I sat down next to Sparky. I could hardly wait for them to return. Would Mary know what the fossil was? Was it really a dinosaur? Would we be famous?

I stood up and paced back and forth, too excited to stay sitting any longer. I glanced at my watch impatiently. Tara had been gone twenty minutes! Why was she taking so long?

Suddenly, Sparky barked and wagged his tail madly. I looked up and saw Tara and Mary running across the beach towards us. Mary was wearing her favourite purple coat and her long brown curly hair was blowing in the wind. She was trying hard to keep up with Tara.

Sparky ran over to greet them, wagging his tail happily. Mary bent down and stroked him affectionately.

"Hello, Peter," Mary panted as she came over. "I hear you've made an exciting discovery!"

"Yes, here it is!" I said, pointing to the boulder.

Mary bent down to examine the fossil.

"What a find!" she exclaimed. "It's a great specimen, beautifully preserved!"

"Is it a dinosaur?" Tara asked excitedly.

"Definitely," Mary replied smiling.

"Yes!" we cried, jumping up and down, delighted at her answer.

"Do you know what sort it is, Mary?" I asked eagerly.

"I can't be sure until we uncover more of the fossil," Mary replied, "but the teeth suggest it was a herbivore."

A plant-eating dinosaur! Perhaps a stegosaurus, with its long bony plates, or maybe an apatosaurus with its huge long neck or...

"Whatever it is," Mary continued, interrupting my thoughts, "it's of great scientific value. Hopefully, the whole skull has been preserved. Let's get it back to the Fossil Shop so we can start work on it straight away!"

"OK," I said, grabbing hold of the boulder.

Tara joined in and we managed to move the boulder slightly.

"It's too heavy," I said. "We won't be able to carry it far."

"Have you got a wheelbarrow, Mary?" Tara asked.

"Yes," she replied, "but I'm not sure it would take the weight and I doubt the three of us could lift the boulder into a wheelbarrow, anyway. I think we're going to need help."

"Professor P!" Tara and I said immediately.

"He's really strong," I added, "and I'm sure he'll have something we can use to move it."

"Good idea," Mary agreed, "I'll wait here with the fossil while you go and find him."

Tara, Sparky and I ran across the beach and up the steps in the cliffs. When we got to the top, Tara and I paused to catch our breath while Sparky continued along the footpath.

"Wait for us, Sparky!" I cried as we sprinted after him.

We raced across the fields and into Farmyard Lane. Sparky ran ahead and waited for us by the gate of an old cottage, overgrown with ivy. On the gate was a faded sign, which read, *Welcome to Honeysuckle Cottage*. Lying on the verge outside the gate was an estate agent's *Sold* board.

"I hope Professor P is in," Tara panted as she pushed open the gate.

"He's probably still unpacking," I said thoughtfully.

Professor P had just moved from Cambridge. We had made friends with him last summer and were so pleased when he decided to come and live here. He was great fun to be with!

As we walked along the moss-covered path to the cottage, I noticed a pile of wooden crates in the driveway. They were marked in big red letters, *Fragile!! Experimental Equipment*.

"I wonder what he's working on?" I said, intrigued.

"Something exciting, I bet!" Tara replied.

The front door was ajar. I pushed it open and we squeezed into the hallway.

"Professor P, are you in?" I called out, through a gap in the pile of removal boxes.

A huge and very hairy dog ran down the stairs and into the hallway to greet us.

"Sleepy!" I cried, stoking her head.

Sleepy was Professor P's wild and very friendly Old English Sheepdog. Sparky dashed over to her, his tail wagging happily. He was delighted to see her again.

"Where's Professor P, Sleepy?" Tara asked, patting her head.

"Woof!" she barked and ran along the hallway to the kitchen.

I gasped in amazement when I opened the door. The kitchen was a complete mess! Bits of electronics, springs, wires and half-finished inventions were scattered all over the floor. The draining board was piled with circuit boards and brightly coloured electronic components. A toaster with wires trailing from the inside lay upside down on the worktop and a beaker of steaming yellow liquid was bubbling on the cooker.

Professor P sat at the table, wearing a white lab coat, splattered with burn marks and yellow stains. He was bending over a circuit board and holding a soldering iron. A suit of armour lay sprawled over the table. Professor P looked up when we came in and smiled.

"Peter, Tara," he greeted us warmly, "and Sparky too. How nice to see you! How are…?"

Before he could finish, Tara burst out, "Professor P! We need your help!"

"Whatever is the matter?" he asked, looking concerned.

"We found a dinosaur!"

"On the beach…"

"It's really big…"

"Can you come now?" I pleaded.

Professor P looked surprised, obviously rather taken aback by our outburst!

"And you need me to help capture it?" he said seriously. "Is it very dangerous?" he added with a smile.

"No, silly!" Tara laughed. "It's a fossil!"

"In that case," he replied, with a twinkle in his eyes. "I would be delighted to help you. What can I do?"

I explained that we needed to get the fossil to Mary's shop and it was too heavy to carry.

"Mary says her wheelbarrow isn't strong enough," Tara added.

"Have you got one we could use, Professor P?" I asked.

"No, I'm sorry, I haven't," he replied. "But perhaps…"

Professor P broke off. He picked up his soldering iron and bent over a small circuit board on the table. Tara and I watched, puzzled, as he soldered a small square chip into the board.

"What are you doing, Professor P?" I asked curiously.

"Inserting the final quantum processor," he replied, too engrossed in his work to look up.

A few moments later, Professor P had finished. He put the soldering iron back in its stand and carefully examined the circuit board.

"That should do the job," he said, satisfied.

Professor P stood up and unscrewed a metal plate in the chest of the suit of armour that was lying on the table. He carefully fitted the circuit board inside the chest compartment and screwed the plate back in place.

"Finished!" he said, pressing a switch on the side of the suit of armour.

He put the screwdriver down on the table and took a step back.

"Peter, Tara, I'd like you to meet my latest invention!" Professor P announced with a dramatic sweep of his hand.

With a loud clanking sound, the armour sat bolt upright.

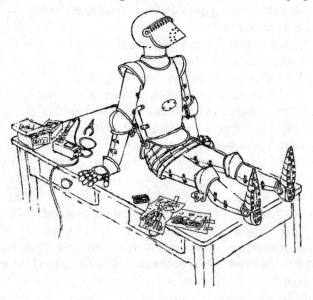

Tara and I jumped back in surprise. Sparky barked nervously and ran out of the kitchen with Sleepy in close pursuit.

"I built this robot to help move all my equipment," Professor P explained. "I haven't had time to finish his computer program but the hardware is ready. He should be able to carry your fossil easily enough."

I chuckled. Nothing as simple as a wheelbarrow for Professor P!

"Robot, I'd like you to meet my friends Peter and Tara," Professor P said proudly.

"Hello," the robot said holding out his leg in greeting.

"Oh, my!" Professor P chuckled, "I must have wired him the wrong way round!"

Professor P removed the panel on the robot's chest and pulled out a handful of coloured wires. He quickly swapped two of the wires and replaced the panel.

"System check, please, Robot," Professor P said.

"All in order," the robot replied.

"Good, now let's try again!"

This time the robot held out his hand.

"Hello," the robot said in a friendly voice.

"Er, hello," I said as I shook his hand. "I'm Peter."

"Pleased to meet you, Peter," the robot replied politely.

"And I'm Tara," Tara added with a giggle.

"I'm…" the robot began. "Who am I, Professor P? Do I have a name?"

"Not yet," Professor P replied. "I'll see if I can think of one later. Right, let's get down to the beach, shall we? We've got a dinosaur to move and we're going to need your help, Robot!"

"A dinosaur!" the robot said nervously. "Aren't dinosaurs big and scary, with sharp teeth and claws and…"

"It's not a living dinosaur!" Professor P chuckled. "It's a fossil."

"A fossil?" the robot said, puzzled. "What's that?"

"It's quite safe, you'll see," Professor P replied encouragingly.

"All right, then," the robot said doubtfully as he climbed down from the table.

We went into the hallway and Professor P grabbed his coat and called to the Sleepy and Sparky. The dogs ran down the stairs, eager to be going outside.

As we were leaving the house, I turned to Professor P and said, "I've just thought of a name for your robot!"

"What's that, Peter?" Professor P asked curiously.

"You could call him Brains!" I said with a chuckle.

Professor P laughed. "Brilliant, Peter!" he exclaimed. "Brains it is!"

"Brains!" the robot repeated proudly. "Yes, that's me!"

CHAPTER THREE

Dinosaur Display

Brains marched happily ahead, so fast we could hardly keep up with him. With each step, he made a loud whirr, clank and click. He swung his arms back and forth, completely out of time with his legs!

"He looks so silly!" Tara said, giggling.

"I hope his arms don't fall off!" I chuckled.

Sparky stayed close to my side, keeping a wary eye on the strange metal creature that was making such odd noises. Sleepy seemed less concerned. She was obviously more used to Professor P's weird and wonderful inventions.

When we arrived at the beach, Brains strode confidently onto the pebbles. Almost immediately he slipped on the wet rocks and toppled backwards

"Help!" he cried, flailing his arms about wildly.

Brains landed on the beach with a loud crash. The noise startled Sparky and Sleepy and they ran off ahead of us.

Professor P, Tara and I rushed over to help Brains back onto his feet.

"The ground went all wobbly, Professor P!" Brains complained pathetically.

"You're just not used to pebbles, yet," Professor P explained. "Go more slowly and you'll be fine."

Supported by Professor P on one side with Tara and me on the other, Brains stepped forwards. He stretched out his arms for balance and cautiously put one foot in front of the other.

"That's it," Professor P said encouragingly. "You're getting it now."

A few moments later, Brains was able to walk without our help. Tara and I left him and dashed on ahead to see

Mary. She was kneeling down beside the fossil with Sleepy and Sparky.

"Hi, Mary, we're back!" we called out to her.

Mary looked up and smiled. She was about to speak when she noticed Brains coming towards her.

"Who... what...?" she stammered, pointing at Brains.

"Good morning, Mary," Professor P greeted her cheerfully. "I'd like you to meet Brains."

"He's here to help carry the dinosaur fossil, Mary," Tara explained. "He's really strong."

Mary looked at Brains doubtfully.

"Well, here's the fossil..." she began.

Before she could finish, Brains marched over to the boulder and effortlessly picked it up.

"Where do you want it?" Brains asked.

Mary's jaw dropped in astonishment.

"Er, to the fossil shop, this way, please" she replied.

Mary led the way across the beach with Professor P and Brains close behind. Tara and I quickly gathered out tools then I called to Sparky and we ran after the others.

I watched anxiously as Brains carried the boulder across the rough ground. One slip and our precious fossil would break.

There was no need to worry. Brains strode confidently across the beach and we soon arrived at the village. Mary unlocked the door of the Fossil Shop and invited us inside.

It was only a small shop but Mary had stocked it with a good range of fossils, crystals, models and books. Tara and I loved spending time in the shop, helping Mary arrange the displays. Recently, we had had great fun making an Easter display in the window with fossil dinosaur eggs.

At the back of the shop was a small room that Mary used for preparing fossils for sale. Mary led the way into the back room and asked Brains to put the boulder down in the middle of the floor.

"Carefully, now," Professor P said as Brains lowered the boulder.

"I did it, Professor P!" Brains said proudly, straightening up again.

"Well done!" Professor P exclaimed, patting Brains on the back.

Professor P knelt down to examine our fossil.

"This is quite a find!" he said, looking very impressed. "Do you know what sort of dinosaur it is?"

"Not yet," Mary replied. "We need to break away more of the rock to…"

"I'll help," Brains burst our eagerly.

He went over to the workbench by the window and picked up a large hammer. He raised it above his head.

"No!" we all cried, in horror.

"I *can* break it," Brains said, looking slightly confused.

"I'm sure you can!" Mary exclaimed.

"That's what we're worried about!" Tara and I added.

"Oh," Brains said, puzzled.

"It's a delicate job, best left to the experts," Professor P explained. "Let's leave it to Peter and Tara, shall we?"

"All right, then," Brains said, reluctantly.

We said goodbye and thanked Brains again for his help. Professor P called to Sleepy and they left the shop. When they had gone, Tara and I started to examine the fossil more closely.

"I'm glad you didn't try to break away the rock with your big chisels," Mary said as she studied the fossil. "We'll need to use my air-pens to remove the rock from around the fossil."

"Air-pens?" I said puzzled.

"Have you ever seen those pneumatic hammers that workmen use to dig up the road?" Mary asked.

"Yes," we replied.

"Well, an air-pen is like one of those but much smaller," she explained. "I'll show you."

Mary went over to the workbench and picked up a pen-like tool attached by a long flexible tube to a large box. She flicked a switch on the box and it sprang into life, making a noise like a vacuum cleaner. Sparky jumped in surprise at the noise and looked at me nervously.

"I think you'll be better off outside, Sparky," I said, taking him into the other room.

When I returned, Mary had put on her goggles and was kneeling down beside the fossil. She touched the end of the pen to the rock and we watched in fascination as it cut into the boulder.

"Do you want to try, now?" Mary asked, after a few minutes.

"Yes!" Tara and I replied eagerly.

"I'll get another air-pen so both of you can work at the same time," she said, going over to the workbench.

"Practice on a part of the rock away from the fossil first, until you get used to it."

I put on my goggles and took hold of the air-pen. I could feel it vibrating quickly in my hand. The tip was moving so fast it was a blur. I carefully put the tip of the air-pen to the rock.

"This is brilliant!" I said as it cut into the rock like a knife through butter.

"The trick is to hold the pen lightly," Mary said as she watched us, "and not to use too much force."

Tara and I gradually learnt to control the air pens as we peeled away the layers of rock,

"I think you've both got the hang of it," Mary said, eventually. "Now, why don't you try closer to the fossil? But be careful not to take off too much of the rock in one go."

I gingerly touched the air pen onto a piece of rock near a tooth. I felt quite nervous – I did not want to ruin our fossil!

"You're doing fine," Mary said, encouragingly. "I'll leave you to it. Come and get me if you need help."

"OK," we replied.

Tara and I bent down over the boulder and continued working. It was great fun, cutting away the rock to gradually reveal the fossil. I felt very excited as we striped away the layers of rock to find more teeth. Eventually, we began to work up from the jaw and we uncovered the dark bony plates that made up the rest of skull.

After hours of careful work, we finished. We put down the tools, stepped back and stared at the fossil. I gasped in surprise. Staring back at me was a dinosaur! I could clearly see an eye socket just above the jawbone and a triangular bump on the top of the head.

"We did it, Peter!" Tara cried excitedly.

"I'll go and get Mary!" I said dashing out of the room.

When Mary came in and saw the fossil, her eyes lit up.

"You've uncovered the whole skull!" she exclaimed.

"Can you tell what sort of dinosaur it is, now?" Tara asked eagerly.

"I'll get my dinosaur book," Mary replied, as excited as we were.

She rushed over to the bookshelf and grabbed a thick black book. Tara and I waited with bated breath as she flicked through the pages.

"Found it!" she said finally.

"You've discovered a scelidosaurus!" Mary announced. "A plant eating dinosaur that lived during the Jurassic Period, about 200 million years ago."

"What did they look like when they were alive, Mary?" Tara asked eagerly.

"Have you heard of a stegosaurus?" Mary asked.

"Yes," Tara nodded, "they're the ones with big bony plates down their backs?"

"And spiky tails," I added.

"That's right," Mary said. "Well, the scelidosaurus was similar to the stegosaurus but with smaller plates. It grew to about four metres in length, that's as long as a car."

"Pretty big then!" I said, grinning.

"You've made quite a find!" Mary exclaimed. "Scelidosaurus fossils are very rare – only a few have been found in the whole world!"

I looked at Tara, delighted. We had done it! We had found a rare dinosaur!

Mary turned back to the book and leafed through the pages.

"Oh, that's interesting," she said. "A scelidosaurus fossil, but one not as good as yours, was found near here a few years ago. It's on display in the Bristol museum."

Mary glanced up from the book and asked, "Have you thought what you'd like to do with your fossil?"

I looked at Tara, unsure.

"There are plenty of collectors and museums who will want to buy it," she continued. "It should fetch a good price…"

"Oh, we can't sell it!" Tara cried, horrified.

"No way," I agreed. "We want to keep it!"

Mary smiled. "I wouldn't want to part with such an amazing fossil either," she said. "But how about putting it on display, so everyone can enjoy it?"

"Good idea," Tara and I agreed.

"We could have an exhibition here if you like," Mary suggested.

"We could call it *The Dinosaurs Display*!" I said proudly.

"And we could make posters for the walls," Tara said excitedly, "to show what life was like when the scelidosaurus was alive!"

"I'll do the writing," I said, "and you could do some of your brilliant drawings, Tara."

"OK," Tara replied.

"You could make a booklet to go with the exhibition," Mary added, "so people will have something to take away with them."

"A *Dinosaur Guide*," I said enthusiastically. "All about Jurassic dinosaurs!"

"Well, that's settled then," Mary said happily. "Let's have a big launch party. I'll invite Dr Simmons and the newspapers." She paused, "And what about the TV reporters too?"

"Brilliant!" Tara and I cried excitedly.

We were going to be famous!

CHAPTER FOUR

The Basement

The next day, Tara called round as I was finishing breakfast.

"Hi, Peter!" she greeted me with a smile as she came into the kitchen. "I made a poster for our dinosaur exhibition last night. Do you want to see it?"

"Yes," I replied enthusiastically, bolting down my last piece of toast.

"It's only a rough sketch," she said, opening her art folder.

Tara put the poster on the kitchen table. At the top of the page, in big bold letters, were the words *Dinosaur Display*. Tara had made the words look as if they had been chiselled out of stone. In the centre of the page, she had sketched our scelidosaurus fossil and drawn fossil shells around the border.

"It's brilliant, Tara," I cried, admiring her work. "I wish I could draw as well as you."

"Thanks," Tara said, modestly.

"I was going to start work on the dinosaur guide last night," I said. "I've got a really good encyclopaedia on DVD with lots about dinosaurs on it. But when I put the DVD in the computer, it wouldn't work. Dad says the disc drive's broken and he's got to send it away to get it fixed."

"Oh, that's a pity," Tara said disappointedly. "It would have been really useful for my drawings too."

I had been really looking forward to working on the dinosaur guide. Now, we would have to wait weeks for my computer to be fixed. Unfortunately, Tara did not have a computer we could use and school was closed for the Easter holidays.

"I know!" Tara said suddenly. "Professor P's got lots of computers. I'm sure he wouldn't mind if we used one of his."

"Good idea," I said cheerfully. "Let's go and see him, now!"

I called Sparky in from the garden and told him we were going to see Professor P and Sleepy. He ran to the front door and barked excitedly!

"Hold on, Sparky," I said, grinning, "I need to get my things first!"

I ran up to my bedroom and picked up the encyclopaedia DVD. Then I raced downstairs, grabbed my coat and scarf and we set off.

As we left the house, I shivered in the icy wind and pulled my coat on tightly. We hurried through the estate to the main road and then crossed into Farmyard Lane. Sparky raced ahead confidently – he knew his way to Professor P's house. When we arrived, Sparky was waiting for us by the gate, wagging his tail happily.

We ran up to the front door and I pressed the bell.

"I didn't hear it ring," I said, trying the bell again.

There was still no sound.

"I think it's broken," Tara said and knocked on the door.

We waited a few moments but there was still no reply.

"He might not be able to hear us if he's in the kitchen," I said thoughtfully. "Let's try round the back."

We walked round the gravel path to the back of the house. I tried the back door and it opened. Sparky dashed inside to look for Sleepy.

"Professor P!" I called out as we went into the kitchen. "Are you in?"

"Professor P is not at home," a voice called out.

I looked round, wondering where the voice had come from. On the sideboard, I noticed a bright orange toaster with its light on. We went over to it.

THE BASEMENT

"Where is Professor P?" I asked the toaster.

The toaster did not reply.

"Do you know where Professor P is, please, toaster?" I said slowly and clearly.

I heard a snigger and turned round but there was no-one to be seen. I looked at Tara, confused, "Who…" I began.

"I don't know why you're talking to the toaster!" the cooker called out smugly. "It's not going to reply. It's just a toaster!"

"And let's hope it stays that way!" the fridge added in a grumpy voice. "There are quite enough of Professor P's 'clever' inventions in my kitchen already."

"Anyone for a riddle?" the kettle piped up brightly.

"Or some philosophy?" the microwave added. "What is the meaning of meaning?" it mused.

"See what I mean?" the fridge complained. "Can't hear yourself think sometimes!"

Tara looked at me and burst out laughing.

"And no, I don't know where Professor P is," the fridge continued, in a slightly offended tone. "He left early this morning and didn't tell me where he was going."

"But you could ask Floppy," the kettle piped up helpfully, "he'll know."

"Where is Floppy?" I asked.

"I'll tell you," the kettle giggled, "but first you must answer these riddles, three. First…"

"Floppy's in the basement," the fridge interrupted dryly.

"Oh, you spoilt it," the kettle cried out disappointedly.

"I didn't think Professor P had a basement…" I began.

"There wasn't a basement when he moved in two weeks ago," the fridge replied. "But he borrowed a digger last weekend…"

"Nearly shook the house down!" the cooker said disapprovingly.

"How do we get to the basement?" Tara asked.

27

"The main entrance is through the garage," the fridge replied, "but that's probably locked, so you'll have to get there through the cupboard under the stairs."

"Thanks," Tara said.

Tara, Sparky and I went into the hall. I opened a small door under the stairway and Tara and I squeezed into the broom cupboard. It was dark, musty and full of cobwebs!

"Stay there, Sparky," I said, pointing to the hallway. "You can't come down into the basement."

He barked indignantly.

"We'll be back soon," I reassured him.

I closed the door behind me and in the darkness, I could see a faint light coming from a hole in the floor. I leant over the hole and called out, "Floppy! Are you there?"

There was no reply.

A metal ladder led down into the depths below. I pulled it to make sure it was secure.

"Is it safe?" Tara asked.

"I think it's OK," I said as I started down the ladder.

Tara followed a few rungs above me. At the bottom, I stepped off the ladder and looked around in amazement. The basement was piled high with parts of old cars, broken fridges, TVs, radios and computers. It looked like a rubbish tip! How on earth had Professor P dug out a basement and filled it with all this stuff so quickly?

As I looked around, I heard a faint banging sound. We threaded our way through the piles of junk towards the noise. I squeezed between two tall freezers and out into an open space. Now I could see just how large the basement was. It was a gigantic cavern with corridors leading out in all directions.

"I think the noise is coming from there," Tara said, pointing to one of the corridors.

Tara and I went into the dimly lit corridor. As we walked along, we passed some doors labelled *Fun Fings*,

Outdoor Oddities, *Gardening Gadgets* and *Just Jokes*. I glanced curiously at them and wondered what was inside.

At the end of the corridor, we turned right and at last, I could see where the noise was coming from. It was Brains. He was swinging a pickaxe at the wall with all his strength. No wonder, nobody had heard us!

I noticed a bright yellow canary sitting on Brains's head. The bird was wearing a miner's helmet and shining the beam of its lantern on the wall.

"Careful, Brains!" the canary cried anxiously. "You almost had the roof down!"

"Sorry," Brains replied.

Tara and I went over to greet them.

"Peter! Tara!" the canary said, turning into a pink fluffy rabbit and grinning.

"Hi, Floppy!" we said cheerfully.

Floppy was Professor P's most brilliant invention. He was actually a supercomputer housed in a small silver ball, but unlike other computers, he did not need a screen or keyboard. Floppy could appear outside the computer as a hologram. He could take any form he wanted and usually looked like a pink rabbit. He had a great sense of humour!

"What are you doing, Floppy?" Tara asked curiously.

"Professor P decided the basement wasn't big enough!" Floppy replied, rolling his eyes in disbelief. "So we're adding a few more rooms!"

"I'm digging a tunnel," Brains said proudly, taking a swipe at the wall with his pickaxe.

"Brains, mind that power cable!" Floppy cried out. "You'll blow the electrics if you're not careful!"

"Oops, sorry, Floppy," Brains said sheepishly.

"So what brings you two here?" Floppy asked with a smile, turning back to us.

"We came to see Professor P," Tara replied. "Do you know where he is?"

"He's gone to Cambridge to get the rest of his things," Floppy replied. "Though, I think he's got quite enough already, don't you?"

Tara giggled at Floppy's disapproving expression.

"Do you know when he'll be back?" I asked.

"Tomorrow," Floppy replied.

"Oh, that's a pity," Tara said disappointedly. "We wanted his help with something."

"What with?" Floppy asked. "Perhaps I can help?"

"We need to look at my encyclopaedia DVD," I explained taking the disc out of my pocket.

"For our dinosaur exhibition," Tara added.

"But my computer's broken," I continued. "So we came to ask Professor P if we could use one of his."

"You could use the one in his study," Floppy said helpfully. "I'm sure he won't mind. I'll help you get it set up, if you like."

"Thanks, Floppy," I said happily.

"Brains, you stay here and keep working," Floppy said in a commanding tone. "We won't be long."

I unclipped Floppy's sphere from Brains' shoulder and we started to walk away. Suddenly, Brains called out anxiously.

"I don't want to be left here all alone," he said. "It's dark. There might be things…"

"Things?" Floppy repeated doubtfully.

"Monsters!" Brains said in a hushed voice.

"If there are any monsters," Floppy said with a chuckle. "I'm sure they'll be more afraid of you! But all right, you can take a break and come with us."

"Thanks, Floppy," Brains said, relieved.

We walked down the corridor and out into the main part of the basement. As we made our way back to the ladder, we passed a huge pile of old and battered looking computers.

"So many computers!" Tara exclaimed. "Why does Professor P need so many?"

Floppy appeared as a fat rabbit in a small white lab coat and wearing big round glasses. He put on a serious expression and imitated Professor P's voice.

"Why, you can never have too many computers!" he said.

Tara and I laughed.

"I wish I had just one!" Tara said wistfully.

"You haven't got a computer?" Floppy cried, throwing up his paws in horror. "That's terrible! How do you manage without one? Professor P couldn't even make a piece of toast without his!"

I chuckled.

"I use the computers at school," Tara said, "and I was hoping to get one for my next birthday…"

"You don't have to wait that long!" Floppy interrupted. "You can have one of these! I'll fix it for you."

"Really!" Tara cried, delighted. "I'd love one!"

"Can I have one too, Floppy?" Brains asked. "I haven't got a computer either!"

"Don't be silly, Brains," Floppy replied. "You don't need one. You're a robot – that's a type of computer!"

"I'm a computer!" Brains exclaimed. "I must be very clever, then!"

Floppy sighed and muttered something under his breath. Then he turned back to Tara.

"Just pick one you like," he said, "and I'll have it going in a jiffy!"

Tara searched eagerly through the pile and found a silver grey notebook computer.

"Do you think I could have this one?" she asked.

"Of course," Floppy replied. "Follow me to the electronics lab and I'll make it into a super supercomputer for you!"

CHAPTER FIVE

Complex Computers

Floppy lead us back the way we had come and then towards a shiny metal door. A large sign on the door read, *No Unauthorised Entry (that means you, Brains!!!)*.

"You can't come in here, Brains," Floppy said firmly. "We don't want you breaking anything again, do we?"

"I won't," Brains protested.

"I'm sure you won't," Floppy said kindly. "But I think it best if you wait here, anyway. We won't be long."

"Oh, all right, then," Brains said reluctantly.

I opened the door and we walked into a long corridor. Unlike the other tunnel, it was well lit and the doors were made of shiny metal. One of them was labelled *Secret Secrets* and another *Dimensional Devices*. Tara stopped at a door with the letters *IDP* written inside a large yellow triangle.

"I wonder what's in there," she said curiously.

Before I had time to reply, Floppy interrupted. "Come along, we're almost there, now."

At the end of the corridor, we reached a door marked *Complex Computers*.

"Here we are!" he announced.

"How do we get in, Floppy?" I asked, pushing the door. "There's no handle."

"It's a Smart Door," Floppy replied. "It will only let in Professor P."

"Well, then, how…" I began.

"Elementary, my dear Peter," Floppy replied.

He disappeared with a pop. Then suddenly Professor P was standing before us! Tara and I gasped in amazement.

Apart from a slightly fuzzy blur around the edges, no one could have guessed he was not the real Professor P.

"Let me in please, Door," Floppy said, imitating Professor P's voice perfectly.

"Hmmm," the door said suspiciously, "you look like Professor P." It paused. "You sound like Professor P. But you must prove you are Professor P. I will ask you a question, so difficult that only Professor P could know the answer."

"Go ahead," Floppy said confidently.

"What is the start of eternity and the end of time?" the door asked mysteriously.

"The start of eternity and the end of time," Floppy repeated, scratching his beard, perplexed. "Very good question, Door. Being an expert in theoretical physics, I believe the answer can be found in quantum field theory?"

The door did not reply.

"Quantum loop theory, perhaps?" Floppy added, trying to sound confident.

"No clues!" the door said tersely.

"I know the answer," Tara whispered to me.

I looked at her in astonishment.

"It's a riddle!" she giggled.

Suddenly, I got it too. It was easy!

"We know the answer, Flop..., I mean, Professor P," I burst out.

Floppy looked at us in surprise. "You do?" he exclaimed. "I didn't know you were experts in theoretical physics."

"We're not," I said, laughing. "It's a riddle, a trick question."

Floppy looked confused.

"The answer is E," Tara whispered. "The letter E is the start of eternity and the end of time!"

"Brilliant," Floppy burst out.

Floppy stood up tall and said in Professor P's most commanding voice, "Open up, Door. I have worked out the answer. It is E."

"Oh, well done, Professor P," the door said happily as it swung open. "I'll see if I can catch you out next time!"

We went into the room and I looked around in surprise. I was expecting it to be messy like the rest of Professor P's house but this was completely different. The room was spotless. Everything was so clean, shiny and well organised.

On the far wall was a long metal workbench neatly laid out with tools – screwdrivers, wire cutters, drills and a soldering iron. On a shelf above the workbench, was an assortment of electronic equipment, shiny boxes with rows of multi-coloured buttons and green display screens. On the wall to the left, was a large cabinet. It looked like an ordinary office filing cabinet but with many smaller drawers.

Floppy appeared as a rabbit wearing a white doctor's coat and holding a stethoscope.

"Let's get to work, shall we?" he said authoritatively, "Put the computer on the workbench and unscrew the back, please, Tara."

Tara picked up a small screwdriver from the workbench. She quickly removed the four screws securing the back of the computer and took off the back cover. We peered inside. I could see a circuit board covered in small black square components with tiny silver wires running between them.

"It looks so complicated!" Tara exclaimed.

"Complicated!" Floppy said scornfully. "Primitive, more like! The processor is years out of date! It will need a complete overhaul to get it up to scratch. We'll need to start by removing the circuit board."

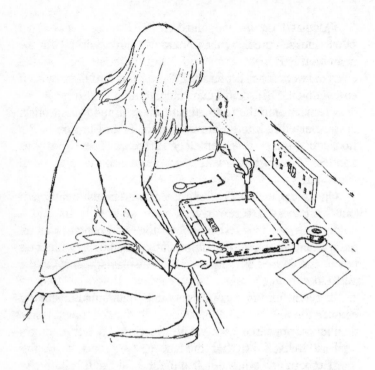

Tara undid the screws holding the board in place. Under Floppy's instruction, she disconnected the various plugs and wires from the board. Then she gingerly lifted out the circuit board, being very careful not to damage it.

"Good work, Tara," Floppy said encouragingly.

"What shall I do with it, now?" she asked, turning the board over in her hands.

"Chuck it in the bin," Floppy replied.

"What?" she burst out in astonishment.

"Oh, it's not worth saving," Floppy said with a shrug. "We're going to build a new circuit from scratch. It's going to be awesome!"

Floppy rolled up his sleeves, "In the electronics cabinet over there, you'll find a blank motherboard."

"A what?" I asked, confused.

"It looks like the circuit board we just took out of the computer," Floppy explained, "but without any of the electronic components on it. We're going to fill the empty sockets on the board with new chips."

I went over to the cabinet and opened it. I pulled out a drawer labelled, *Motherboards* and took one out.

"You'll need to insert the computer chips into the sockets," Floppy explained. "First, the CPU."

"What's a CPU?" Tara asked.

"It's the Central Processing Unit," Floppy explained. "It's the brain of the computer."

Using a pair of tweezers, I took one of the square chips out of the cabinet. It was slightly smaller than a fifty pence piece and it sparkled like silver holographic wrapping paper.

"It's one of Professor P's special quantum computing chips," Floppy explained proudly. "It works much faster than an ordinary one."

Tara carefully placed the chip into a socket on the motherboard and clipped it into place.

"This is easy!" she said, happily. "It's like Lego!"

Under Floppy's expert guidance, Tara inserted more chips into the motherboard. Finally, only one empty socket remained.

"Almost done," Floppy said excitedly. "The last one is the network chip – it will enable you to connect to the internet."

I pulled opened the drawer in the cabinet marked, *Network Chips*. Inside was a small black box with the letters *QED* written in bright gold letters on the lid.

"Is this the right box?" I asked, "the QED one?"

"QED!" Floppy exclaimed in surprise. "Professor P never mentioned to me that he was working on a QED!"

"What's a QED?" I asked.

"It stands for Quantum Entanglement Device," Floppy replied. "It's a type of network that works instantly, without radio waves."

I opened the box and saw two chips resting on a black silk cloth. I picked up one of the chips and looked at it closely. It resembled a glass marble that had been cut in half. Inside, I could see tiny swirling pinpricks of light. On the inside of the lid, written in bold red letters, were the words, *WARNING! EXPERIMENTAL & UNTESTED.*

"Is it OK to..." I asked as I read the label.

"Yes, yes," Floppy interrupted. "Professor P puts warnings on everything. I just ignore them! Put it in the computer, Tara and we'll see what it does!"

"Won't Professor P mind?" Tara asked, unsure. "He's only got two chips..."

"Trust me, Tara," Floppy replied, smiling reassuringly. "He'll be only too happy for us to try out one of his new chips, and besides, he's got a spare."

I felt slightly uneasy as I watched Tara fit the chip into the circuit board.

"All done!" Floppy said proudly. "Now put the circuit board back into the computer and switch it on.

A few moments later, Tara had put the computer back together. She pressed the power button and we waited expectantly as the computer started up.

A message appeared, *Checking system... diagnostics complete... system OK.* Then, with a fanfare, a message flashed onto the screen, *WELCOME TO YOUR SUPER SUPERCOMPUTER!!*

"It's working!" Tara cried, delighted. "Well done, Floppy!"

"My pleasure," Floppy said, taking a bow.

"Put in your DVD, Peter," Tara said eagerly. "Let's see if it works."

I put the DVD in the drive and a message appeared, *An update may be available for this program. Do you want to update now?*

Tara clicked on *Yes* and another message appeared, *Attempting to connect to the internet. Initialising Quantum Entanglement Device...*

The screen went blank. Moments later, it filled with flashing dots, like coloured snow. We watched the dots dance hypnotically around the screen.

"I think it's crashed," I said after a few minutes of nothing happening. "Do you think we should switch it off?"

"No," Floppy replied. "It might damage the hard drive. Let me connect directly to the computer and I'll see if I can find out what's going on."

I put Floppy's sphere next to the computer. He hovered in front of the screen and peered at it intently.

"Hmmm," he muttered, "very interesting."

"Is the computer all right?" Tara asked anxiously.

"I think so," Floppy replied, cautiously. "The problem seems to be with this new Quantum Entanglement chip. It's trying to connect to a computer network and not succeeding. I'll see if I can sort it out..."

A look of deep concentration appeared on Floppy's face. He gradually began to fade, looking misty, almost like a ghost.

"Fascinating!" he cried. "Absolutely fascinating!"

"What is it, Floppy?" I asked curiously.

"The computer has found something amazing..." Floppy began. "I'm trying to help it decode the network signals, they're encoded, you see and I've never come across anything quite like them before..."

Floppy vanished. I looked at Tara, bewildered. What was going on?

On the computer's screen, a pattern began to form in the dots. They began to move together to form horizontal lines. Finally, a message box popped up on the screen, *Signal decoded. Please log in to the IGW.*

Floppy appeared as an owl, grinning from ear to ear.

"I did it!" he cried. "I got us onto the IGW! I can't wait to tell Professor P!"

"What is the IGW?" Tara asked, confused.

"You'll see in a moment," Floppy replied. "First you need to log on. Enter your full name and address."

"My full name and address?" Tara repeated.

"Oh, it's just a formality, hurry up now, please, Tara," Floppy said impatiently.

Tara typed in her details, *Alicia Tara Royce, 129 Seaview Close, Seatown, Dorset.*

A message appeared, *Welcome Alicia Tara Royce, you are now logged on to the IGW.*

"We've done it!" Floppy cried. "We're logged onto the IGW. This is the biggest thing since…" he paused. "Actually It's the biggest thing ever!"

"What is?" I asked, bewildered. "I thought the computer was just going to update my encyclopaedia DVD…"

"Your DVD!" Floppy said in a dismissive tone, "I think we can do better than that! Let's see what I can find out about dinosaurs on the IGW."

Suddenly web pages started to flash up on the screen. I noticed some dinosaur pictures but the pages disappeared to quickly for me to read them.

"Slow down, Floppy!" Tara cried. "We can't read it!"

"I'm trying," Floppy replied, "but the data is coming in too fast…"

Pages continued to flash up on the screen.

"I don't believe it!" Floppy cried. "This is amazing, everything you could possible want! You'll love it, Tara…"

Tara looked at me, puzzled. "Love what?" she began.

"I'll explain in a moment," Floppy replied, "just as soon as I get the speed problem sorted."

The screen was flashing on and off so fast it became a blur. Then suddenly, Floppy disappeared and the screen went dead.

I watched in horror as a plume of black smoke billowed out of the computer!

"It's on fire!" Tara cried as flames rose up from the keyboard.

I quickly grabbed the power lead and wrenched it out of the computer. Tara ran over to the door and grabbed a small red fire extinguisher. She pointed it at the computer and a jet of foam shot out, engulfing the keyboard.

The flames disappeared and we stared in horror at the burnt out remains of the computer. It was completely ruined.

"Oh, no!" I burst out. "Tara, look!"

I pointed to Floppy's sphere. A trickle of smoke was coming from it.

Floppy had burnt out too!

CHAPTER SIX

The Unexpected Egg

"Floppy!" I cried in dismay. "Are you all right?"

Floppy did not reply. I picked up his sphere but dropped it quickly. It was burning hot.

"What are we going to do?" Tara asked her face white with shock.

"We'll have to call Professor P," I replied, "and tell him what's happened. I've got his mobile number at home."

"I hope he can fix Floppy," Tara said staring at the burnt out sphere.

We left Floppy sphere in room and ran back along the corridor. As I rushed out into the main part of the basement, I tripped over Brains who was lying in front of the door.

"Brains!" I cried as I picked myself up. "What are you doing!"

Brains did not reply.

"Are you all right, Brains?" Tara asked anxiously.

Brains still did not reply. I bent down and noticed a small red light on the side of his neck, blinking on and off.

"I think he's broken, too!" I said, surprised.

"Come on, Peter," Tara urged. "We've got to talk to Professor P!"

We left Brains lying on the floor and climbed up the ladder out of the basement as fast as we could. When I opened the door into the hallway, Sparky ran over, wagging his tail madly.

"Come on, Sparky!" I called, "We've got to go home, now!"

"Woof!" Sparky barked and bounded over to the front door.

We dashed out of the cottage and raced home. Breathless, we arrived at my house. I fumbled for my key, flung open the front door and we rushed up to my bedroom. I grabbed my mobile phone and quickly dialled Professor P's number.

Ring, ring, ring. I looked at Tara and shook my head. There was no reply!

I was just about to give up when I heard Professor P's friendly voice answer the phone.

"Hello, Peter," Professor P said. "Sorry, to take so long, but I…"

"Professor P!" I burst out. "Thank goodness, you're there!"

"Is everything all right?" Professor P asked, concerned.

"No!" I replied. "We were at your house, there was a terrible accident! The computer caught fire! Floppy burnt out! And Brains is lying on the ground, broken!"

I paused to take a breath.

"Are you and Tara all right?" Professor P asked quickly.

"Yes, we're fine," I replied.

"Good," Professor P said, relived. "Now tell me exactly what happened," he continued in a calm reassuring voice.

Professor P listened carefully as I explained everything. Finally, I said goodbye and put the phone down

"What did he say?" Tara asked anxiously. "He wasn't cross with us was he?"

"No, he says not to worry," I replied. "He's sure he'll be able to fix Floppy and Brains."

"Oh, thank goodness," Tara said, breathing a sigh of relief.

"Oh, and he said he'll give you another computer," I added, "one that works properly this time!"

"Brilliant!" Tara said happily.

I felt so relieved after speaking to Professor P. He was not cross with us and I knew he would be able to mend Floppy and Brains.

"What shall we do now?" I asked as I sat down on the bed, exhausted.

"Well, I'm starving," she replied, "let's have lunch. Then afterwards we could make a start on our dinosaur guide, I've got a few books at home we could use."

"OK," I said, feeling hungry too.

"Woof!" Sparky agreed.

After lunch, we went round to Tara's house. We went upstairs to her bedroom which, as usual, was very neat and tidy – unlike mine!

By the window was a desk and to the left of it, a bookshelf. Tara went over and took three books down from the shelf.

"Here are my dinosaur books," she said. "They're a bit basic, but the pictures are good."

"Oh, they're fine," I said, enthusiastically as I flicked through the pages.

"Let's start by deciding which dinosaurs to put in our guide," Tara suggested.

She opened the desk drawer and took out a notepad and pens. She gave me the notepad and I wrote at the top of the page, *Dinosaur Shortlist*.

"First choice – scelidosaurus!" Tara said.

"Definitely!" I agreed, writing it down.

We went through the books and made notes as we tried to find the best dinosaurs to include. As I scribbled on the pad, Sparky kept running over to me, wanting to play.

"Not now, Sparky, we're busy," I said, pushing him away gently. "We'll take you for a walk later," I added, stroking his head.

Sparky finally seemed to understand and wandered out of the bedroom, looking for someone else to play with.

Half an hour later, he returned. He came over and nuzzled against my leg.

"Hi, Sparky," I greeted him, "we're almost finished."

As I reaching down to stroke him, I noticed he had something in his mouth.

"What have you got there, Sparky?" I asked, curiously.

"Woof," Sparky barked and dropped a parcel at my feet. He looked up at me with a very pleased expression and wagged his tail proudly.

I picked up the parcel. It was about the same size as a shoebox and wrapped in silver paper.

One corner was slightly wet where Sparky had been holding it in his mouth. I wiped the corner with my sleeve, turned it over and saw a printed label. It read, *Alicia Tara Royce, 129 Seaview Close, Seatown, Dorset.*

"It's for you, Tara," I said, giving it to her.

"For me?" she said surprised. "I wonder what it is."

Tara turned the box over in her hands.

"It's wrapped up so well I can't even see the join in the paper!" she exclaimed.

Tara pulled open the desk drawer, took out a pair of scissors and cut into the wrapping paper. She pulled hard at the paper and it suddenly ripped, spilling tiny silver polystyrene balls everywhere. Most of them landed on Sparky!

"Sorry, Sparky," Tara apologised.

Sparky shook himself vigorously, sending balls flying everywhere.

"Oh, Sparky!" I laughed. "Now, look what you're done!"

I got down onto my hands and knees and scooped the silver balls into the wastepaper basket. Tara emptied the rest of the packaging material from the parcel into the bin. Inside the parcel was a round object covered in silver bubble wrap. Sparky came over and sniffed at it eagerly.

"It's an Easter egg!" Tara said happily.

Tara quickly pulled off the bubble wrap to reveal a grey speckled egg about the size of a small grapefruit. She looked at it, puzzled; it was not the chocolate Easter egg she expected!

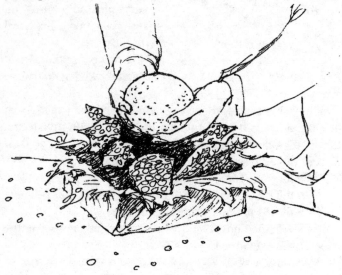

"What do you think it is?" Tara asked, passing it to me.

I ran my hands over the ball. It felt quite smooth to the touch.

"It looks like one of those plastic dinosaur eggs Mary sells in her shop," I said thoughtfully.

"It must be from Mary then, for our exhibition," Tara said confidently.

"Yes, of course," I agreed. "It'll look great!"

"We could make a nest for it..." Tara suggested.

"With some leaves and ferns," I added.

"Good idea," Tara said happily. "Let's go and see Mary now to thank her."

Tara put the egg back in the bubble wrap and placed it in her rucksack. I called to Sparky and we set off, down the hill to the village. When we arrived at the Fossil Shop, Mary greeted us with a warm and friendly smile.

"Hi, Mary," Tara said cheerfully. "Thanks for the egg, it's great!"

"The egg?" Mary repeated, blankly.

"The dinosaur egg," Tara replied.

"What dinosaur egg?" Mary asked.

Tara took the egg out of her rucksack and showed it to Mary.

"Where did you get this?" Mary asked, taking hold of the egg.

"It was sent to my house," Tara replied.

"We thought it was from you, Mary," I added, "for our exhibition."

"No, it's not from me," Mary said, shaking her head.

I glanced at Tara, puzzled.

"It's very well made," Mary said as she examined the egg. "Very realistic – I've never seen one quite like it before. I should sell these in the shop. Was there a note with it? A packing slip?"

"No," Tara replied. "Nothing."

"There's some writing on the egg," Mary continued. "It's so small I can hardly read it, but I think it says, *Universal Reptile Repository*. I've never heard of them but I'd like to get their catalogue..."

"If you didn't send it to me, Mary," Tara interrupted. "Then who did?"

"One of your relatives?" Mary replied.

"I suppose so," Tara said doubtfully.

"Your mum probably forgot to give it you at Easter," I added, "but Sparky went and found it."

Sparky wagged his tail and look up at me proudly.

"Well done, Sparky" Tara said, patting him on the head. "I'm happy to have an extra Easter present! And it'll look great in our dinosaur exhibition!"

"Yes, it will," Mary said, pleased. "I've just been sorting out the back room, ready for the exhibition. Come and have a look."

We followed Mary into the back of the shop. She had cleared away her tools and everything was now clean and tidy. Our scelidosaurus fossil was in the middle of the room, lying on a low table covered with a black velvet cloth.

"It looks brilliant," I said as we went over to look at it.

"I rang Dr Simmons last night," Mary said, smiling, "and he rushed over to look at your fossil. He says it's one of the best preserved specimens he's ever seen!"

I looked at Tara, delighted.

"He says you've made an important discovery," Mary continued, "and scientists will be able to learn a great deal from studying your fossil."

"That's fantastic!" I cried.

"I told him about your exhibition too," Mary continued, "and he's looking forward to seeing it."

"We need to make it really good, then," Tara said, looking round the room, thoughtfully. "Let's make a nest for the dinosaur egg on that shelf, over there by the window."

"Good idea," Mary said encouragingly. "And I've got just the thing to go with your egg."

She left the room and returned a few moments later with handful of baby dinosaur models

"Oh, they're great!" I said, picking one up.

"I'm glad you like them," Mary smiled.

"They're so lifelike," I said. "It looks like they're just hatched!"

"We can put them around the outside of the nest," Tara added, "and then…"

The bell above the shop door tinkled.

"Sorry, I'll have to see to my customers," Mary interrupted. "I'll leave you to it. You can find plenty of leaves for your nest in the courtyard outside."

Tara and I went through the back door into the courtyard. With Sparky's help, we gathered plenty of leaves and twigs. We made a nest out of the sticks on the shelf above the radiator and then filled it with leaves. Tara carefully placed the egg on the leaves and stood back to admire it. Sparky jumped up, trying to get a look too. I picked him up to show him what we had done.

"You like that egg, don't you, Sparky?" I said. "We'll have to get you one!"

"Woof!" he barked eagerly.

We arranged the baby dinosaur models around the nest and were just finishing when Mary returned.

"It looks so realistic!" Mary exclaimed. "You've done a great job."

"Thanks, Mary," we said, proudly.

"I'm going to close up the shop now," Mary continued, glancing at her watch, "but do call round tomorrow and we can do some more work on the exhibition."

"Thanks, Mary, see you tomorrow," we replied happily.

The sun was going down as we left the shop and I shivered in the cold wind. We walked as fast as we could up the hill and arrived home just as it was getting dark.

"Bye, Peter, bye Sparky," Tara said as she went into her house. "I'll call round early tomorrow!"

"Bye, Tara," I said. "See you tomorrow."

Sparky and I went into my house. I had only just taken off my coat when the phone rang.

"Peter," Tara said. "I just had to ring you. It's about the dinosaur egg."

"What...?" I began.

"My parents don't know where it came from either," she burst our.

"So who sent it to you, then?" I asked mystified.

"I have no idea!" Tara replied.

CHAPTER SEVEN

Dotty

"Morning Peter!" Tara said cheerfully as she came into the hallway. "I think I've worked out where the egg came from!"

"Where?" I asked.

"Professor P must have sent it," Tara replied. "He's the only person it can be. No one in my family knows anything about it. And Professor P knew about our dinosaur find."

"Yes, that makes sense," I nodded.

"Let's go and ask him about it later, when we've finished at Mary's" Tara said.

"Good idea," I agreed.

"Are you ready to go to Mary's now?" Tara asked.

"OK," I replied. "I'll just get Sparky."

I called Sparky in from the garden and grabbed my coat from the hallway. We walked briskly along the estate road and then raced down the hill to the village. As we made our way across the village green to the Fossil Shop, I heard a car toot behind us. I looked round and saw Mary in her old Morris Minor. We waved to her and ran over to the car. Sparky jumped up at the window to see who was inside.

"Hello," Mary greeted us warmly as she wound down the window.

"Hi, Mary," I replied, "we were just coming to see you."

"Well, that's good timing," she said. "I haven't opened the shop yet, I'm running a bit late. I'll park the car and see you there in a moment."

We waited outside the shop until Mary came over. She took a large bunch of keys out of her handbag and opened the door. Sparky ran in first and started barking madly.

"Oh, no!" Mary cried as she entered the shop.

Tara and I looked inside and gasped in shock. The room was in a terrible state!

Fossils and shells were strewn all over the floor and the shelves were in a dreadful mess.

"I've been burgled!" Mary exclaimed. "My lovely shop…" she broke off, too upset to continue.

Mary bent down and picked up a large shell.

"Broken," she said quietly, tears welling up in her eyes. "A beautiful nautilus shell. Smashed to pieces…"

"We'll help clear up, Mary," Tara said kindly, reaching down to pick up a fossil from the floor.

Mary shook her head.

"Not yet, thank you, Tara," she replied tearfully. "We mustn't clean up until the police have been. They'll need to search for fingerprints."

Sparky ran around sniffing everything curiously.

"He's got the scent," I said confidently. "You'll catch them won't you, Sparky?"

"Woof, woof," he barked and ran over to the door leading into the back room.

The door was ajar. Sparky pushed it open and we quickly followed him into the room. Our scelidosaurus fossil was still on the table in the centre of the room, just as we had left it.

"Oh, thank goodness they didn't take your fossil!" Mary exclaimed. "It's the most valuable thing in the shop. I suppose it must have been too heavy for them to carry…"

"But they've taken the egg!" Tara burst out.

The nest we had made yesterday had been knocked off the shelf. A pile of leaves and twigs lay in a heap on the floor. There was no sign of the egg.

"Who would want to steal a toy egg?" I said, confused. "It doesn't make sense!"

Sparky was working his way around the room, sniffing at everything. He reached the outside door and I went over to join him.

"I don't think they got in this way," I said, examining the door carefully. "The lock isn't broken."

"We'll have to leave it to the police to find out," Mary said, in a calmer voice. "I'll go and call them now."

Mary returned to the main part of the shop to make the call. Tara and I continued looking around the room, trying to work out how the shop had been entered. We examined the windows closely but could find no sign of damage.

"It's very odd," I said, puzzled. "How did they get in?"

Before Tara could reply, we heard a loud scream from Mary, "Help!" she called out. "Help!"

Tara and I rushed into the main part of the shop. Mary had her hands to her mouth. Her face was white. She looked terrified.

"What is it, Mary?" I cried.

"Ra...Rat," she stammered. "A rat. I saw the tail..."

"Where?" Tara screamed.

"Over there," Mary pointed, her hand shaking. "It ran behind the counter."

"Sparky!" I called out. "Come here!"

Sparky dashed into the shop and ran over to join me.

"Rat, Sparky!" I said. "Find it!"

Sparky cocked his head and looked around the room eagerly, waiting to pounce on anything that moved.

"No, Peter!" Mary warned. "It's too dangerous! What if Sparky gets bitten? Rats can carry terrible diseases..."

I quickly grabbed hold of Sparky's collar. I certainly did not want him to get hurt!

"We'll have to leave the shop," Mary said. "I'll call the pest control people and let them deal with it."

"Woof! Woof!" Sparky barked loudly.

He broke loose from my grip and before I could stop him, he raced towards the counter. He tried to jump onto it but it was too high for him to reach.

"There!" Tara cried suddenly.

She pointed to a shelf above the counter that had a collection of plastic dinosaur models and toys on it. I looked closely but could see no sign of the rat.

"What did you see, Tara?" I asked.

"Th...there!" Tara stammered. "Look, Peter!"

I looked again to see what she was pointing at. In the centre of the shelf was something that looked slightly different from the other models. It was green and yellowy brown in colour and had a shiny rubbery skin.

"No!" Mary cried in astonishment.

"What is it, Mary?" I asked, wondering what was going on.

Then, out of the corner of my eye, I noticed something move. I looked up at the shelf again and saw the little brown creature flick its tail. It was not a model – it was alive!

I jumped back in surprise as the creature scrambled along the shelf. It knocked one of the dinosaur toys onto the floor and then leapt onto the counter.

Sparky barked excitedly and jumped up at the counter, trying desperately to reach it.

"No, Sparky!" I yelled, pulling him back.

I held tightly onto his collar. The creature ran in confusion to the edge of the counter and back again. Finally, it froze in the middle of the counter and stared at us with its large green eyes. It looked very frightened.

"Don't get any closer," Mary said cautiously.

"What is it?" I asked.

"I don't know," Mary replied. "It looks like some kind of lizard. I'll see if I can capture it before it runs away again."

She picked up an empty cardboard box and walked slowly towards the creature. As she approached the counter, the animal backed away nervously.

"The poor thing's terrified," Tara whispered.

"It's all right," Mary said gently, "we're not going to hurt you."

Then she quickly placed the box over the creature.

"Got it," she said, with a sigh of relief.

Mary ripped a hole in the top of the cardboard box and we peered inside.

"So, was it you who did all this damage?" Mary asked the creature.

"Eeek! Eeek!" it cried, looking at her with its large pleading eyes.

"There's no need to be afraid," Mary said as she reached into the box and carefully took it out.

The little creature lay peacefully in Mary's hands. It looked calmer now.

"Do you know what it is, Mary?" I asked.

"Some sort of reptile, I think," she replied. "You can tell that from the scaly skin."

Tara and I peered closely at the creature. Its rough skin had no trace of hair.

"I think it might be an iguana," Mary added, thoughtfully.

"An iguana?" Tara repeated.

"That's a type of lizard," Mary continued. "They're often bright green in colour…"

"Oh, yes, I know," I said. "They have them in the pet shop in Bridport."

"I can't imagine how it got into the shop," Mary continued, puzzled. "It looks like it's just hatched."

"Just hatched?" I repeated.

"My egg!" Tara exclaimed, suddenly. "It must have come from my egg!"

"Let's check," I said, rushing into the back room.

Tara quickly followed me into the room. We knelt down to inspect the remains of the nest under the shelf. Sure enough pieces of broken egg shell were mixed in with the leaves!

"It's true, Mary!" Tara said as we ran back into the shop. "It did come from my egg."

"So you're the proud owner of an iguana then!" Mary said, passing the creature to Tara.

Tara held out her hands and nervously took hold of the little creature. It gently nuzzled her hand and looked up at her trustingly.

"Oh, it's really cute," Tara said, as she stroked its head gently.

"It certainly seems friendly enough," Mary agreed.

"Do you think it's a girl or a boy, Mary?" Tara asked.

"I'm not sure," Mary replied. "You'll have to take it to the vet, to find out."

"I think she's a girl," Tara said, confidently.

Mary smiled.

I reached out and touched the creature. She felt surprising warm and soft, not at all slippery. The underneath of her body was pale brown. She had dark green and brown stripes on her back and brown spots on her nose. She peered at me with large friendly green eyes and flicked her long tail.

Sparky looked up at the creature and wagged his tail too.

"You want to make friends, don't you, Sparky?" I said, smiling.

"Woof!" he barked playfully.

"Oh, what a wonderful Easter present!" Tara said, delighted. "I always wanted a pet of my own!"

"What are you going to call her?" Mary asked.

"What about Dotty?" I suggested, "because she's got brown spots on her nose."

"Dotty!" Tara said with a chuckle. "Yes, I like that! I'll call her Dotty!"

"You'd better check with you're parents that you can keep her," Mary said, concerned.

"I'm sure they won't mind," Tara replied. "Let's go and see my mum now, Peter. We can ask her to take us to the pet shop too. We'll need a book on iguanas and some toys too, and a playhouse and…"

Mary laughed.

"Sounds like you're going to be very busy!" she said.

Mary carefully took the creature from Tara and put it back in the cardboard box. She poked some air holes in the top and sealed the box securely with plenty of tape.

"It's amazing that such a small creature could cause so much mess," Mary said as she gave the box to Tara, "but at least it wasn't burglars!"

"Or rats!" I added.

"I'm sorry about the damage, Mary," Tara apologised. "Can we help you clear up?"

"No, that's OK," Mary replied kindly. "I won't keep you. I expect Dotty is probably getting hungry."

"Thanks, Mary," Tara said gratefully, as she put Dotty's box into her rucksack.

We were just about to leave the shop, when Mary said, "I can't see you until the weekend. I'm off on holiday for a few days but I'll be back on Saturday. We can do some more work on the exhibition then."

"We'll have to make a new nest," Tara said, "but with a plastic egg this time!"

"Definitely!" Mary chuckled.

"See you Saturday, then," she said as we went over to the door.

"Come on, Sparky!" I called out. "We're going to the pet shop!"

"Woof!" Sparky barked happily.

"Bye," Mary called as we rushed out of the shop. "Have fun with your new pet, Tara!"

CHAPTER EIGHT

Forgetful Floppy

As we made our way home, Tara skipped along happily, chatting excitedly about Dotty. She was so pleased to have a pet at last!

I was really glad for Tara but I kept wondering where the iguana had come from. Why would Professor P send it to her? And without asking first? It made no sense!

Tara did not seem concerned, though. She was just delighted to have Dotty.

When we arrived at Tara's house, she flung open the door and called out excitedly, "Mum, are you in?"

Tara's mother came down the stairs. She had fair hair like Tara's, but it was short and curly. She was holding a duster in one hand and a can of polish in the other.

"Is everything all right, Tara?" she asked, concerned.

"Can we go to the pet shop?" Tara burst out.

"The pet shop?" her mother repeated, puzzled.

"You know that egg I told you about," Tara said. "It's real! It hatched! And out came Dotty! Mary thinks she might be an iguana…"

"An iguana!" her mum exclaimed. "Isn't that a type of lizard…?"

"Let me show you," Tara interrupted. "Dotty's really cute! You'll love her!"

Tara took the cardboard box out of her rucksack and put it on the table in the hallway. Sparky wagged his tail eagerly and I picked him up so he could see more clearly.

Tara opened the box and gasped in horror. Dotty was lying at the bottom of the box, pale and lifeless.

"Dotty, are you all right?" Tara cried as she quickly reached into the box and took out the little creature. "Oh, you're frozen!"

Dotty opened her eyes and looked up at Tara pathetically.

"Eeek!" she whimpered meekly.

"I'll get a warm towel," Tara's mother said, rushing into the kitchen.

She returned a few moments later. Tara wrapped Dotty in the towel and held her close to her chest.

"I hope she's going to be all right," Tara said anxiously.

"Lizards are cold blooded," Tara's mother explained. "They can't keep warm like us. But I expect she'll soon warm up."

Moments later, Dotty poked her head out of the towel. She looked around curiously and flicked her tail playfully.

"See, she's fine now," Tara's mother said, reassuringly.

"I can keep her, can't I, mum?" Tara pleaded.

Tara's mum hesitated. "Well, I know you really want a pet…"

"I do!" Tara burst out.

"All right then," Tara's mother said with a smile.

"Thanks, mum!" Tara cried. "Can we go to the pet shop now? There're lots of things we need to buy for her…"

"We can't, it's half day closing today," her mum interrupted, shaking her head. "We'll have to go tomorrow."

"Oh, no!" Tara said disappointedly.

"She'll be all right till tomorrow," Tara's mother said kindly. "We can get everything she needs then."

"All right," Tara agreed, reluctantly.

"By the way," Tara's mother added. "Have you found out who sent you the egg, yet?"

"Professor P," Tara replied confidently. "I told him I wanted a pet. He must have wanted to surprise me!"

"How kind of him," Tara's mother said. "That reminds me, he called just after you left. He says he's fixed your computer and you can pick it up anytime."

"Great!" I said excitedly. "Let's go round there now, shall we, Tara?"

"OK," Tara replied. "I can thank him for Dotty. But I don't want to risk taking her out into the cold again..."

"Don't worry, Tara, she'll be fine here," Tara's mother reassured her. "I'll look after her while you're away."

"Thanks, mum," Tara said happily.

Tara carefully put Dotty back in the cardboard box. The little creature lay peacefully on the towel, almost asleep. She gave the box to her mother and we dashed off with Sparky to Professor P's house.

When we arrived at Honeysuckle Cottage, I knocked on the front door. A loud voice boomed out at us and we jumped back in surprise.

"Welcome to Professor P's residence!" the door said in a pompous voice. "Come in, Peter, Tara and Sparky."

"Thanks," we said, slightly taken aback.

"Professor P is expecting you," the door said as it sprang open. "He is in the computer room in the basement."

As we went into the hallway, the door added sternly, "Remember to wipe your feet."

"Professor P's fixed the door, all right!" I whispered and Tara giggled.

Sleepy bounded down the stairs to welcome us. Sparky wagged his tail and the two dogs dashed out into the garden together.

Tara and I went down into the basement and made our way to the *Complex Computer* room. The door was ajar and we went inside. Professor P was sitting at the workbench, holding Floppy's sphere in one hand and a screwdriver in the other. Professor P looked up and smiled as we came into the room.

"Peter, Tara," he greeted us, "How nice to see you."

"Hi, Professor P," we chorused.

"Thank you so much for Dotty!" Tara burst out. "I love her! She's the best present you could have given me!"

"Dotty?" PP repeated, puzzled.

"Yes, that's what I decided to call her," Tara replied.

"Who?" Professor P asked.

"The iguana you sent me," Tara replied.

"The iguana?" Professor P repeated, blankly. "I'm afraid I don't know anything about an iguana"

"Didn't you send me the egg then, Professor P," Tara asked.

"No," he replied. "It wasn't from me."

Tara looked at me baffled.

"Well, where did she come from, then?" she asked.

I shrugged. It was a complete mystery.

"Anyway, let me just finish this," PP said, turning back to Floppy's sphere. "I need to make one final adjustment to Floppy's circuit."

"Is he going to be all right?" Tara asked, concerned.

"Let's find out," Professor P replied.

We watched in silence as Professor P fitted a tiny circuit board inside the sphere and screwed on the cover.

"Done," Professor P said finally. "Let's see if Floppy's working correctly, shall we?"

Professor P tapped the sphere twice and Floppy appeared as a pink rabbit. He had a bandage around the top of his head, half covering his large floppy ears and a sad expression on his face.

"Are you all right, Floppy?" Professor P asked, concerned.

"No," Floppy replied pathetically. "I've lost my memory."

"Have you forgotten everything?" Professor P asked.

"I don't know," Floppy replied, shaking his head slowly. "I can't remember what I can't remember."

Professor P chuckled. "What's the last thing you do remember?" he asked kindly.

"Going into the computer room with Peter and Tara," Floppy replied. "After that everything is blank."

"I don't think that's too serious," Professor P said, winking at us. "I'm sure you'll be fine!"

"I suppose so," Floppy admitted grudgingly. He obviously wanted a lot more sympathy!

"And what about Brains?" Tara asked, "Is he all right, Professor P?"

"Yes, he's fine, now," Professor P replied. "I left him working in the garden, digging my vegetable patch."

"He's not as sensitive as I am," Floppy whimpered and blew his nose with a large red handkerchief.

"Do you know what went wrong with Brains?" I asked.

"I don't know exactly what caused it," Professor P replied, "but there was a sudden power surge which damaged the main computer network. Brains is linked to the network, you see, and that's what caused him to lock up. Nothing serious fortunately!"

"Well, that's a relief," Tara sighed.

"My condition is much more serious, you know," Floppy continued. "But fortunately I'm brave…"

"Yes, most fortunate," Professor P interrupted, winking at us. "Why don't you have a rest now, Floppy?"

"I think I will," Floppy said with a sigh. "It will help to calm my nerves."

Professor P chuckled and turned to us. "Would you like to see your new computer, now, Tara?" he asked.

"Yes, please," Tara replied eagerly.

Professor P reached up to one of the shelves and brought down a silver notebook computer.

"Here it is," he said putting it on the workbench.

Professor P opened the lid and switched on the computer.

"Welcome, Tara," the computer greeted her in a warm friendly voice.

"It talks!" Tara said, delighted.

"Delighted to be of service!" the computer said proudly.

"I hope you have fun with it, Tara," Professor P said, smiling.

"Oh, it's brilliant!" Tara cried. "Thank you so much Professor P! Now, Peter and I can get on with out dinosaur guide."

"You're welcome," Professor P said as he began packing the computer away into a black case.

As we were starting to leave the room, Floppy suddenly burst out, "Don't leave!"

We stopped and looked at Floppy, concerned.

"What is it Floppy?" I asked.

"I remember coming in here yesterday and fixing Tara's computer," Floppy cried excitedly. "Then something amazing happened..."

Floppy broke off, looking confused.

"What happened, Floppy?" Professor P asked curiously.

"I don't remember exactly," Floppy replied, "I know it had something to do with your QED chip. I used one of them to fix Tara's computer."

"You used one of my special QED chips!" Professor P exclaimed.

"I'm sorry, Professor P..." Tara apologised

"Floppy said it was OK..." I added sheepishly.

"Floppy," Professor P said sternly. "It took me a year to design that QED chip. It cost a small fortune to have two of them made! I haven't even had a chance to try them out. And now you've blown one of them up!"

"Sorry, Professor P," Floppy said, meekly chewing one of his ears.

"Well, at least there's one left," Professor P said with a sigh.

"Try it now," Floppy urged. "Something really fantastic happened before, honestly, Professor P."

"OK, let's find out then," Professor P said, his curiosity aroused.

As Professor P went over to the electronics cabinet, Floppy burst out excitedly, "I just remembered something else! I saw a huge swirling mist. And millions of tiny lights. Everything was joined to everything else."

"Really," Professor P said, distractedly as he gathered a handful of electronic components.

"Yes, it was awesome!" Floppy continued. "It was all one. Everything was one!"

Floppy's voice trailed off. As he gazed into the distance, Tara whispered to me, "Do you think he's OK?"

I shrugged, not quite sure. Floppy did act strangely sometimes but I had never seen him quite like this before.

"Well, that's the basic circuit finished," Professor P announced, moments later.

Professor P had attached a screen, keyboard and mouse to the motherboard and plugged chips into most of the empty sockets. Only one empty socket remained.

"Now for the QED chip!" he said proudly

"What does the QED chip do?" I asked, intrigued.

"It lets computers talk to each other in a whole new way," Professor P replied. "It's called Quantum Entanglement."

"Quantum what?" Tara said, puzzled.

"Imagine you had a piece of paper, Tara, a very special piece of paper," he said, "and Peter had one too. And whatever you wrote on your piece appeared instantly on his, no matter how far apart you were. That's Quantum Entanglement!"

"That would be amazing!" I gasped.

"Like magic!" Tara added.

"Yes, it does sound like magic, doesn't it?" Professor P chuckled. "But it is science, trust me. Soon all computers will use QED chips to connect to the internet. It won't matter how far away the computers are from each other, they'll all be linked instantaneously."

That sounded fantastic! I felt a thrill of excitement – Professor P had invented a new super-fast internet! What an amazing discovery!

"To see a world in a grain of sand..." Floppy said dreamily.

Then he stopped and gazed at us knowingly.

Professor P chuckled. "Very poetic, Floppy!"

Professor P turned back to the circuit and made a few final adjustments.

"I'll run a basic system check," he said when he had finished.

Professor P flicked a switch on the power supply and typed some commands into the keyboard. A message appeared on the screen, *Diagnostic complete. System functioning correctly.*

"All in order," Professor P said, satisfied. "Let's try it now, shall we?"

"Yes!" we cried excitedly.

CHAPTER NINE

IGW

We watched in anticipation as Professor P typed at the keyboard. What would his new chip do? I wondered excitedly.

"It's ready," Professor P announced after a few moments. "When I press the enter key the QED chip will power up."

Professor P pressed the key and the screen went blank. Moments later, it filled with flashing dots, like coloured snow. Professor P looked at the screen and stroked his beard thoughtfully.

"Strange," he said puzzled.

"It did that before," I said, "and we thought it had crashed."

"But Floppy got it working," Tara added.

"I did?" Floppy said in surprise. "I wonder how? I must have done something very clever, something only a super-intelligent super-computer like me could think of..."

Professor P cleared his throat loudly.

"When you do finally remember," he said, "perhaps you could enlighten us. Until then..."

"Of course, Professor P," Floppy replied. "No, wait something's coming...Yes, I see three letters!"

"Do you happen to know what these letter are, Floppy?" Professor P asked with a sigh.

"They were..." Floppy hesitated. "The letters W, I and G!"

"Wig?" Professor P repeated doubtfully.

"No, it was IGW!" I burst out excitedly.

"That it, IGW!" Floppy agreed.

"And what does IGW stand for, exactly?" Professor P asked.

"I don't remember," Floppy replied mournfully, "but give me a few suggestions and I'll see if it jogs my memory."

"International Green Week," Professor P replied, "Increased Gross Weight, Investment Grade Wine, Internal Gravity Waves. Am I getting close, Floppy?"

"No, no, no and no," Floppy said, shaking his head, despondently. "None of those. It was something to do with... Everything was connected, like a web."

"The World Wide Web?" Professor P asked.

"No, it was bigger than that..." Floppy broke off, deep in thought.

Tara looked at me concerned. Was Floppy OK?

"Got it!" Floppy burst out suddenly. "I remember what the IGW is! In fact, I remember everything! Let me connect directly to the computer and I'll show you."

"I don't want you to have another accident, Floppy," Professor P said, looking doubtful. "In your current state..."

"I'll be fine," Floppy interrupted excitedly. "Trust me, Professor P," he pleaded.

"All right, but be careful," Professor P urged.

Professor P put Floppy's sphere next to the circuit board. Floppy hovered in front of the screen and peered at it intently, just as he had last time. Tara and I waited anxiously, worried that Floppy might burn out again.

After a few moments, Floppy said, "I've decoded the quantum signals. You'll see what's going on, now. Turn off the lights, please!"

Professor P went over to the switch and turned off the lights. It took a while for my eyes to adjust to the semi-darkness of the room.

We all turned to look. A swirling spiral of mist appeared before us.

"What is it?" I asked, puzzled.

"Our galaxy, the Milky Way" Floppy explained. "Over a hundred thousand million stars! I'll zoom in so you can see more clearly."

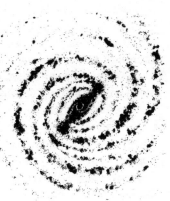

The Milky Way grew larger. Now, I could clearly make out one of the spiral arms. It was made up of countless pinpricks of light and joining them were tiny glowing lines, like a spider's web.

"Now do you see, Professor P?" Floppy announced ecstatically.

"Not really," Professor P replied, puzzled, "What's this got to do with..."

"It's a network!" Floppy explained. "A gigantic web of quantum entanglement!"

"Good heavens!" Professor P exclaimed in amazement. "Are you sure?"

"Yes," Floppy insisted. "There's no doubt!"

Professor P sat down in his chair, a stunned look on his face.

"Professor P, I don't understand..." I began.

"See these pinpricks of light," Floppy said. "They're planets, all linked by a vast computer network."

Tara looked at me, totally bewildered.

"What...?" she began.

"It means," Professor P said slowly, "there must be life on these other worlds!"

"Intelligence life!" Floppy burst out excitedly. "Extraterrestrials! E.T.s. Bug eyed monsters! Aliens!"

I stared at Tara in disbelief.

"Aliens?" Tara repeated incredulously.

"Yes, aliens," Professor P nodded. "We are not alone. There are aliens on other planets, all talking to each other via one huge network, the Intergalactic Web."

"And we're about to join the party!" Floppy cried.

I looked at the swirling image of the Milky Way in astonishment. Could it really be true?

"In a few moments we're going to make contact with aliens!" Professor P said excitedly.

Professor P switched on the light and sat back down at the workbench. He tapped away intently at the keyboard, briefly stopping to have a technical discussion with Floppy. I glanced at Tara questioningly. Were we really about to communicate with aliens from outer space?

"Do you think it's safe, Peter?" she whispered nervously.

"I hope so," I said, not quite knowing whether to be excited or terrified.

"That should do it!" Professor P said finally. "You can disconnect now, Floppy, I think I've solved the stability problem. I'll download the translation engine and we'll be up and running in a moment."

Professor P's hands flew over the keyboard again. Suddenly, a loud trumpeting sound boomed out and a message appeared on the screen, *Welcome to the Intergalactic Web – your Gateway to the Galaxy!*

Underneath the heading, were moving banners and flashing signs:

G–Search – Find anything in over 100 million planets!

G–Bay – Buy and sell anything in the known Galaxy – instant teleport delivery!

G-Know – All the knowledge in the galaxy available at the click of a button!

"You've done it, Professor P!" Floppy cried, turning somersaults in the air. "It's working!"

I felt a surge of excitement. There really were millions and millions of stars and galaxies out there, full of aliens!

"Oh, where to begin?" Professor P said, rubbing his hands excitedly. He looked like a child with a new toy! "So much to discover, so little time!"

Before he had time to start, an advert popped up on the screen, *Doodleclams – buy one, get ten free! With our latest Doodleclam you'll never need to worry about Burbletops again!*

"Burbletops!" Tara giggled. "I wonder what they are?"

"Well, I'm not going to worry about them," Professor P chuckled as he closed the advert. "Let's see what we can find out in the knowledge database."

He clicked on the button at the bottom of the screen and a new page appeared.

Welcome to G-Know – the finest source of knowledge in the galaxy.

History - from the Big Bang to the Big Crunch.

Literature – top Billion Books discussed

Science – Astronomy to Xenobiology, if you can't find it in our database it's not worth knowing!

"Let's start with science, shall we?" Professor P said, eagerly.

He clicked on a link and a new page appeared. The heading read, *University of Alpha Centauri, Science Foundation Course.*

"I don't know where to begin!" Professor P said eagerly as he scrolled through the pages.

Tara and I looked on bewildered as Professor P scanned pages of mathematical equations, muttering excitedly to himself. Floppy was equally thrilled. He had turned into an owl and was flapping around, unable to contain his excitement!

"Look Professor P, there's the M-Theory formula!" Floppy cried joyfully.

"And the Quantum gravity equations," Professor P added, delighted. "Everything I ever dreamed of! It would take mankind hundreds of years to discover all of this!"

"See if you can find the dimensional formula," Floppy suddenly burst out, "for the IDP!"

Professor P nodded excitedly. "Good idea, Floppy!"

"What's the IDP?" Tara asked curiously.

"My latest invention," Professor P said distractedly as he scanned through the pages. "It's…I'll explain later… Ah, here we are!"

"That's it!" Floppy exclaimed. "You found it, Professor P!"

"So simple!" Professor P whistled. "Let me check it."

Professor P quickly took a pen out of his jacket pocket then frantically searched his other pockets and pulled out a crumpled envelope. He scribbled down the equations, muttering excitedly to himself.

While Professor P was making notes, I noticed a faint smell of burning.

"Professor P," I began.

"One moment, Peter," he replied. "Almost finished."

"But, Professor P," I continued. "I think something's burn…"

BANG!

The noise was deafening! The QED chip exploded in a puff of smoke! Professor P reached for the power supply and quickly switched it off.

Floppy put his hands over his ears and shook his head in dismay. "Oh no!" he wailed. "Not again!

"Don't worry, Floppy," Professor P said his eyes shining with excitement. "We've got the formula – that's what counts!"

"So now we can get the IDP to work?" Floppy asked eagerly.

"Definitely!" Professor P replied.

Professor P stood up abruptly. "Peter, Tara, if you will excuse me, Floppy and I have work to do!"

"We're going to be *very* busy!" Floppy added seriously.

Professor P handed Tara her notebook computer.

"Thank you, Professor P," she said, delighted.

"You're most welcome, Tara," Professor P said, smiling.

Tara and I left the basement. I called to Sparky as we went into the front garden and he ran over to me, his tail wagging happily.

The light was fading as we walked home through the woods. I watched Sparky darting through the trees chasing leaves, blissfully unaware of what had just taken place. When we arrived home, I turned to Tara, still not quite able to believe what I had seen.

"Did that really happen?" I asked, still feeling bewildered. "Did we just make contact with aliens?"

"I guess so," Tara replied.

I looked up at the evening sky. The stars were just beginning to appear. I stared at them and wondered what amazing creatures lived there.

And I knew we were not alone.

CHAPTER TEN

Teething Troubles

The next morning I woke up to the sound of knocking on my door. I sat up in bed and looked around, bleary eyed. As I rubbed the sleep from my eyes, my mother poked her head round my bedroom door.

"Morning, Peter," she said cheerily. "Tara's on the phone."

"Thanks, mum," I said, stumbling out of bed.

I put on my dressing gown, went downstairs and picked up the phone.

"Hi, Peter," Tara greeted me. "Can you come round?"

"Sure," I replied, sleepily.

"I've just got back from the pet shop," Tara added. "I bought lots of things for Dotty."

"Great," I said, yawning, "Just give me a few minutes to get dressed and have breakfast."

"OK, see you soon," Tara said happily and put down the phone.

When I arrived at Tara's house, she was very excited.

"Hi, Peter, come in!" she said, "Do you want to see what I got from the pet shop?"

Before I had time to reply, she rushed me into the kitchen and proudly said, "Look! I bought a large cage for Dotty. She can sleep in it at night. She'll be safe in there."

"That's a good idea," I nodded.

"I also bought a book on reptiles," Tara added, "and a tub of vitamins. The man in the pet shop said to sprinkle a little vitamin powder on her food.

"She needs vitamins?" I said surprised.

"To give her strong bones," Tara replied. "Oh, and I got a food bowl too."

"Do you know what she eats?" I asked.

"Fruit and vegetables," Tara replied. "I tried giving her a piece of apple last night but she wasn't hungry. The man in the shop said Iguanas don't eat much after they've just hatched. I expect she's hungry now though, I'll go and get her."

Tara left the kitchen and returned a few moments later carrying Dotty's cardboard box. Tara put the box on the kitchen table and took out Dotty. The little creature looked around the kitchen curiously.

"Let's get you something to eat, Dotty," Tara said as she went over to the fridge.

She put a lettuce leaf, a carrot and a piece of apple into Dotty's bowl. Then she then sprinkled a little of the vitamin powder on top. She put the bowl on the table beside Dotty.

Dotty ate a piece of lettuce and quickly spat it out again. She looked up at Tara, wide-eyed.

"Don't you like it, Dotty?" Tara said, concerned.

"Eek, eek!" Dotty whimpered.

"Maybe she doesn't like the vitamin powder," I suggested.

"I probably put on too much," Tara said, taking the bowl over to the sink. "I'll wash it off."

Tara rinsed the food and put it back on the table. This time, Dotty nibbled at the lettuce contentedly.

As Dotty munched away on the leaves, I picked up the book Tara had bought from the pet shop. It was called *Reptile Care* and had a picture of a large green Iguana on the front cover. Inside were photos of different kinds of lizards of all colours and sizes. Some had weird horns on their heads and looked like aliens from space! I flicked through the pages, curious to find out what type of iguana Dotty was.

When I reached the end of the book, I looked at Dotty, puzzled.

"Tara," I said tentatively. "Are you sure Dotty is an iguana? I can't find any like her in here."

I gave the book to Tara and she glanced at the photos.

"I don't think she's green enough," I continued, "and her neck's too long."

"Yes, you're right, Peter," Tara said, puzzled, as she turned the pages. "She doesn't look like any of these lizards."

"Dotty's legs look different too," I added. "Hers are straight. The iguana's legs are bent, like they're squatting."

"I suppose I should have taken her to the pet shop with me," Tara said thoughtfully. "They would have known what sort she is. But I didn't want to risk taking her out in the cold again."

Suddenly, Dotty began to choke.

"Eeek! Eeek!" she cried, looking very pale.

"Dotty! Are your all right?" Tara cried out.

Dotty swallowed a few times and then was sick all over the table!

"What's the matter, Dotty?" Tara asked anxiously.

"We'll have to take her to the vet," I said concerned. "I think she's ill."

"But mum's gone out!" Tara said, tears welling up in her eyes. "She went to pick up Rosie and I'm not sure when she'll be back!"

Tara picked up Dotty and cradled her in her hands. I got a cloth from the sink and started to clean the sick from the table. Just as I was finishing, I heard the sound of the front door opening.

"Oh, thank goodness, mum's home!" Tara said relieved.

She put Dotty back in her box and we dashed into the hallway. Tara's mother stood in the doorway, with Rosie,

Tara's little sister. Rosie was about five years old with long blond ponytails and freckles.

"Mum, Dotty's ill?" Tara burst out. "We need to take her to the vet!"

"What's wrong with her?" Tara's mother asked, concerned.

"She's been sick!" Tara replied, "Come and see."

Tara's mother followed us back into the kitchen.

"Oh, no!" Tara cried, glancing at the box. "She's gone!"

I looked around – Dotty was nowhere to be seen!

"Where are you, Dotty?" Tara called out.

Out of the corner of my eye, I saw something move. I turned and saw Dotty dart out of the kitchen! We followed her into the hallway and then into the living room. Tara quickly closed the door behind us.

Where had Dotty gone? I glanced around and noticed a large rubber plant in the corner of the room. One of its branches was swaying back and forth!

"There she is!" I said, pointing to the rubber plant.

Dotty had climbed half way up the plant and was gnawing at the leaves!

"She's trying to eat it!" Tara's mother exclaimed.

Tara dashed over and reached out to grab Dotty. The little creature jumped down off the rubber plant and ran along the floor. Tara's mother bent down and quickly scooped her up.

"Got you!" she said.

"Can we take her to the vet's now, mum?" Tara pleaded.

Tara's mother examined Dotty closely.

"Her eyes look bright enough," she said reassuringly. "She doesn't look ill to me, Tara."

"But she was sick," Tara insisted, "after she ate a piece of lettuce."

"Maybe it was the wrong type of food for her," Tara's mother said kindly. "Why don't you try and see if she'll eat some other food? Maybe some leaves from the garden?"

"OK," Tara agreed, "but if she's sick again, can we take her to the vet's?"

"All right," her mother replied, giving Dotty back to Tara.

As Tara's mother left the living room, Rosie came into the room.

"Can I play with your new pet, Tara?" she asked, going over to look at Dotty.

"Not now, Rosie," Tara sighed, "we need to get her something to eat."

"Can I stroke her, then?" Rosie asked sweetly.

"All right," Tara agreed, lowering her hands.

"I didn't know you had a pet dinosaur, Tara!" Rosie said, surprised.

Tara laughed. "Dotty isn't a dinosaur, Rosie. She's a type of lizard…"

"No, she's not!" Rosie insisted. "She's a dinosaur!"

"Dinosaurs are extinct," Tara began to explain. "They all died out a very long time ago…"

"But I've got one!" Rosie said, running out of the room.

"Rosie's dinosaur mad!" Tara explained to me.

Moments later, Rosie reappeared, clutching a soft dinosaur toy.

"Look!" she cried. "Dippy the dinosaur!"

"Dippy's just a toy, Rosie," Tara said patiently. "She's not a real dinosaur…"

"But Dotty is!" Rosie cried, tugging Tara's arm. "I'll show you!"

We followed Rosie upstairs into her bedroom. I chuckled when I saw the room – Rosie really was dinosaur mad! She had dinosaurs wallpaper, dinosaur curtains and a dinosaur duvet cover. Above her bed was a dinosaur mobile and on her chair was a pop-up dinosaur book.

Rosie went over to her toy box and took out a large picture book. She quickly turned the well-thumbed pages until she found what she was looking for and then she thrust the book at Tara.

"See!" Rosie cried, triumphantly.

I peered over Tara's shoulder to look at the illustration in the book. It showed a forest scene of pine trees and ferns. Half buried in leaves on the forest floor was a group of about a dozen eggs. A small creature was climbing out of one of the broken eggs.

I looked closely at the creature and gasped in surprise. It was the same as Dotty!

Tara read out the title of the illustration, "Baby diplodocus hatching in the forest."

"I told you!" Rosie said proudly. "Dotty's a dippy-loddy-cus!"

Tara turned to me, a look of confusion on her face.

"Peter…" she began. But then she broke off, speechless.

BABY DIPLODOCUS HATCHING OUT OF EGG ON FOREST FLOOR...

I felt equally astonished. Dotty could not be a dinosaur! They all died out millions of years ago. She must be some other type of reptile, one that was not in Tara's book.

"I think we should have a look on the internet to find out what Dotty is," I said thoughtfully.

Tara agreed. "We can use my new computer," she added.

Tara and I left Rosie in her bedroom, happily playing with Dotty and her dinosaur toys. We went into Tara's bedroom and sat down at the desk. Tara switched on the computer.

"Hello, Tara!" the computer said brightly. "How can I help you today?"

"Are any dinosaurs alive?" Tara asked.

"No," the computer replied firmly. "According to my database, all the dinosaurs died out at the end of the Cretaceous Period, approximately 65 million years ago."

"That's what we thought," Tara said, turning to me. "Dotty must be a lizard, then, Peter."

I nodded. "I wonder what type of lizard she is. Computer, do you know how many types of lizard there are?" I asked.

"Four thousand, eight hundred different species," the computer replied instantly.

"That's a lot!" I said surprised. "It'll take us ages to search through them all."

"I can do that for you," the computer said helpfully. "I can take a picture of her with my webcam and then search the internet to find the best match."

"Good idea," Tara said enthusiastically. "I'll go and get Dotty."

Tara dashed out of the room and returned a few minutes later with Dotty. She held Dotty up to the computer's webcam.

"Please rotate her slowly," the computer said, "so I can get an accurate 3D image of her."

Tara turned Dotty around in front of the camera. Dotty kept squirming and it took a few minutes before the computer was satisfied.

"Done," the computer said finally. "I have a complete scan. Now, I can begin searching the internet databases."

Tara and I watched in anticipation as hundreds of pictures quickly flashed up on the screen. A few minutes later, the computer spoke.

"I have found a perfect match," it said confidently.

"Great, what sort of lizard is Dotty?" Tara asked eagerly.

"Dotty is not a lizard," the computer replied. "I must apologise for misinforming you earlier. There must be a mistake in my database."

"What do you mean?" I asked, confused.

"Dinosaurs are obviously not extinct," the computer replied.

"Not extinct?" Tara repeated.

"No," the computer continued, "because Dotty is a dinosaur. She is of the species *Diplodocus longus*, common in the Late Jurassic, 155-145 million years ago."

I looked at Tara in utter astonishment. Dotty a real dinosaur!

But how?

CHAPTER ELEVEN

Dotty Dilemma

"There must be a mistake!" Tara said, confused, "Dotty can't be a real dinosaur."

"I am not mistaken," the computer replied firmly. "Observe the images closely."

On the left of the screen was a rotating 3D image of Dotty. Through her half-transparent outline, the computer had drawn her skeleton like an X-ray picture. On the right of the screen was another skeleton labelled, *baby diplodocus fossil.*

I looked at the two pictures closely. They were exactly the same!

I read the fact file on the screen at the bottom of the screen.

Species: Diplodocus longus
Adult Size: 27 metre long
Adult Weight: 15 tonnes

"Fifteen tonnes!" I exclaimed. "That's enormous!"

"It is approximately the weight of three elephants," the computer added helpfully.

"But…" Tara began. "I still don't understand… How can she be a real dinosaur? Dinosaurs are extinct!"

"Maybe scientists have found a way to bring dinosaurs back to life…" I said thoughtfully.

"But if that was true it would be in all the papers and on the news!" Tara interrupted.

"I suppose it would," I agreed, "but perhaps it's only just happened."

"Computer, can you check?" Tara asked. "Have scientists worked out a way to bring back the dinosaurs?"

"Searching internet research papers…" the computer replied.

Tara and I waited impatiently as pages flashed up on the screen. A few minutes later, the computer spoke.

"Scientists are currently trying to recreate dinosaurs through genetic manipulation of bird DNA," the computer said. "But they do not expect to succeed for at least five years."

"Well, where did Dotty come from then, Peter," Tara said, puzzled.

I shrugged, equally confused.

"Eeek! Eeek!" Dotty cried out suddenly.

The little dinosaur looked up at Tara with pleading eyes and nibbled her hand gently.

"Oh, Dotty, you must be starving," Tara said kindly. "We'll get you something to eat soon. Computer, can you find out what Dotty eats, please?"

"Of course, Tara," the computer replied helpfully.

A few moments later, a webpage flashed up on the screen. We read it eagerly.

Diplodocus Diet: Adult diplodocus mainly eat pine leaves. They swallow the leaves whole, without chewing and have very long guts, which enable them to digest the tough leaves.

"That's a relief," Tara said. "There are plenty of pine trees around here."

"Just a minute, Tara," I said as I scrolled down the screen. "Read this!"

Young diplodocus have smaller guts and are unable to process such indigestible plant material. Instead they eat the softer leaves from cycadeoid plants.

At the bottom of the page was a picture of a small shrub with a thick trunk and long fern like leaves. Dotty jumped up and tried to bite the computer screen.

"That's what you want to eat isn't it, Dotty?" Tara said, gently pulling her away from the computer.

"It looks like a palm tree," I said, peering at the plant.

"We might be able to get one at the plant shop in the village," Tara suggested. "They sell potted rubber plants and I think they might have palm trees too."

"Good idea," I agreed.

Tara picked up her notebook. She wrote down the name of the plant and quickly drew a sketch of it.

"That should do," Tara said, satisfied. "Let's go, Peter."

"Oh, before you leave," the computer said. "I have some additional information which..."

"Tell us when we get back, computer," Tara said, jumping up.

"But I believe this information is highly..." the computer began.

Tara picked up Dotty and we quickly left the room. We went into Rosie's bedroom and Tara gave Dotty to Rosie.

"Will you look after Dotty, please Rosie?" Tara asked. "We're going to the shop to get her some food."

"OK," Rosie said happily.

"Bye, Dotty," Tara called out as we left the room, "see you soon."

We left Tara's house and went round to mine to pick up Sparky. He dashed out of the house wagging his tail, happy to be going out for a walk. We raced along the estate and down the hill to the village. At the florist's shop, I put Sparky on the lead and we went inside. We were greeted by an older woman with grey hair tied up in a bun.

"Good Morning, how can I help you?" she asked with a smile.

"Do you have one of these?" Tara asked, showing the sketch to the woman.

"Let me see," the florist replied. She put on her glasses and peered carefully at the drawing. "No, but I have some decorative ferns…"

"It's got to be exactly the same as this one," Tara insisted, pointing to the picture. "A cycadeoid."

"A cycadeoid?" the woman said, puzzled. "I've never heard the name before. Do you want me to see if I can order one for you?"

"Will it take long to arrive?" Tara asked anxiously.

"I can probably get one delivered tomorrow," the florist said helpfully. "That's if my suppliers have one. Let me check my catalogues."

She reached under the counter and brought out a set of thick books. She opened one of them and turned to the index at the back.

"That's odd," she said as she leafed through the pages. "I can't find any mention of *cycadeoid*. Let me try my other suppliers."

We waited anxiously as she slowly worked her way through all the catalogues.

"Oh, dear," she said finally. "I'm afraid no one stocks any cycadeoids."

"No one!" Tara said, looking very upset.

"Well, if it's important…"

"It is!" Tara insisted. "We really need one as soon as possible. It's life or death!"

The woman looked at Tara, puzzled.

"We've just had a new computer system installed," she said. "I've not quite got to grips with it yet, I'm afraid. But I could try and find a specialist supplier on the internet."

"Oh, yes, please," Tara said, gratefully.

The woman swivelled her chair round to face the screen. She picked up the mouse and clicked it a few times.

"I think it's working," she said as she hesitantly typed on the keyboard.

Tara looked at me nervously as we waited for her to finish.

A few minutes later, the woman swivelled her chair round and looked at us sternly.

"Is this a joke?" she asked suspiciously.

We looked at each other in surprise.

"No!" I said indignantly. "It's not a joke. We really need a cycadeoid."

"Can't you find it?" Tara asked anxiously.

"Oh, I've found it all right," the woman replied. "Look here," she pointed to the screen.

I read aloud, *Cycadeoids are characterized by thick trunks and compound leaves. They first appeared in the Triassic Period and were very common in the Jurassic Period. At the end of the Cretaceous they became extinct.*

"Extinct!" Tara cried in horror.

"Yes," the woman replied. "It looks like they died out a long time ago. Are you sure you don't want a fern instead."

Tara looked horrified. She was too shocked to reply.

"No thank you," I stammered.

"I'm sorry I couldn't help," the woman said, concerned.

"Thanks for trying," I added.

We left the shop and walked across the village green.

"What are we going to do?" Tara asked anxiously.

I did not reply. Tara sat down on a bench and put her head in her hands.

"Are you all right, Tara?" I asked, sitting down beside her.

"No!" she sobbed. "No, I'm not all right!"

Sparky looked up at Tara concerned. Why was she so upset? He made a whining sound and nuzzled against her leg.

I put my hand on Tara's shoulder. "We'll think of something, Tara," I said gently.

"But what?" she wept. "If there's nothing for Dotty to eat, she'll starve!"

CHAPTER TWELVE

Explanations

We sat on the bench in silence. I did not know what to say to Tara. I felt dreadful. If we could not find something for Dotty to eat soon, the poor little creature would starve.

I kept trying to make sense of what had happened. If Dotty was a real dinosaur, where had she come from? Who sent her to Tara? Whoever sent her must know where to get food…

BOOM!!

I jumped in surprise as a loud bang filled the air. Sparky jumped up and barked, the hair on his back standing up on end.

"What was that?" Tara cried.

"I don't know," I replied, startled.

"It can't have been thunder!" Tara said, looking up at the clear blue sky.

"It sounded more like an explosion!" I said, jumping up. "And I think it came from over there," I added, pointing in the direction of the beach. "Let's have a look."

Tara wiped the tears from her face with her coat sleeve and stood up. We rushed across the village green and over to the beach car park. I scanned the beach. It was deserted.

"Look, Peter!" Tara said suddenly, pointing out to sea.

About half a mile away was a small island covered in trees. I could just make out a cloud of yellow smoke above the island.

"An explosion on the island!" I said in surprise. "What could have caused it?"

Tara shook her head, equally puzzled.

The island was too small for anyone to live on and it had no buildings. I could see no sign of life on it either. No boats were moored and the whole island looked completely deserted.

A sudden flash of yellow light burst from the island, followed, a few seconds later, by another loud bang.

"What do you think it is, Tara?" I asked.

"I've no idea!" she replied, equally confused.

We waited for another ten minutes but nothing else happened, so we decided to go home. Tara fell silent again as we walked up the hill. When we reached the estate, she looked at me, her eyes puffy with tears.

"What are we going to do about Dotty?" she asked distraught.

I looked down, not knowing what to say. We had tried the florist, there was no point in going back to the pet shop and Mary was away. Who could we turn to?

"We could go and see Professor P," I said thoughtfully. "He might know someone who could help. Maybe a professor at his old University, a plant expert."

Tara's face brightened.

"OK," she said hopefully.

With Sparky running ahead, we raced up the hill and through the woods to Professor P's house. When we arrived at the cottage, I raised my hand to knock on the front door.

"Professor P is not in the house," the door said, before I had a chance to knock.

"Do you know where…?" I began.

"No, I do not," the door replied indignantly. "He did not inform me of his plans. Good day."

I glanced at Tara. She looked terribly disappointed – Professor P was our last hope. As we turned to leave, Sparky ran over to the garage at the left of the house. The garage had obviously seen better days; the walls were thickly encrusted with ivy and the green paintwork on the door was flaking away. As we went over, I heard a banging sound coming from inside.

"Professor P," I called out as I pushed the door. "Is that you?"

The banging stopped and the door opened. Brains stood in the entrance, holding a large hammer in his hand.

"Brains, do you know where Professor P is?" Tara asked urgently.

"I wish I did," Brains replied anxiously. "I finished all the jobs he gave me ages ago. Now, I don't know what to do. So, I was banging nails into the walls. I like banging."

I chuckled. Brains could be so silly sometimes!

"When did you last see Professor P?" Tara asked.

"Yesterday afternoon," Brains replied. "He went off with Floppy in the car. Professor P said they were going to do an experiment. Floppy said it was dangerous. I hope they didn't have an accident."

"Do you know where they went?" I asked, concerned.

"To..." Brains paused, trying to remember, "an island..."

"An island?" I exclaimed. "Tara, you don't think..."

"That explosion!" she interrupted.

"Explosion!" Brains burst out. "Oh, no! Professor P has had an accident! He's blown himself up."

"I'm sure he's alright..." I began, trying to reassure Brains.

"I'll never see Professor P again!" Brains wailed. "Oh, what am I going to do?"

"Let's call the coastguard, Peter," Tara suggested, "and tell them what we saw."

"Good idea," I agreed.

We ran over to the house and I knocked loudly on the front door.

"Let us in, please, Door," I said. "It's urgent! We need to use the phone."

"Password?" the door boomed.

"We don't know the password!" Tara said, frustrated.

"In that case, you will have to wait for Professor P to come back," the door said firmly.

"Open up!" Brains cried, hammering at the door with all his strength. "Professor P has had a terrible accident. He needs our help!"

"An... an accident!" the door stammered. "You'd better come in right away!"

The door swung open. We were just about to go inside when I heard the sound of a car behind us. I turned round and saw Professor P in a red open-top vintage car. He drove into the gravel driveway and slammed on the brakes. I had never been so pleased to see him!

"Peter, Tara!" Professor P called out cheerfully. "How nice to see you!"

We ran over to greet him. I laughed when I saw how he and Floppy were dressed. Professor P was wearing a black leather-flying jacket and an old-fashioned pair of goggles. Floppy was perched on Professor P's shoulder, dressed the same way. Sleepy was sitting in the passenger seat with her paws resting on the dashboard. Her tongue was hanging out and her long hair was covering her face!

"Oh, thank goodness you're all right, Professor P," Tara burst out.

"We heard an explosion..." I said hurriedly.

"We thought you'd had an accident," Tara added.

"I thought I'd never see you again, Professor P," Brains whimpered pathetically.

"Don't worry, Brains," Professor P chuckled as he pushed his goggles onto his forehead. "I'd never leave you!"

"Thanks, Professor P," Brains said happily.

"But what was that explosion?" I asked.

"Nothing to worry about," Floppy replied knowingly, "all part of the plan!"

"Plan?" I repeated, looking at Professor P, puzzled.

But Professor P did not reply. He noticed Tara's red, swollen eyes and looked at her concerned.

"Is everything all right, Tara," he asked kindly.

Tara looked down, embarrassed.

"Why don't you come into the house?" Professor P said gently, as he climbed out of the car. "We can have a drink and a biscuit and you can tell me all about it."

"Thanks, Professor P," Tara said quietly.

We went into the kitchen and Professor P put three glasses of juice and a plate of biscuits on the table.

"Now, Tara," Professor P said, as he sat down at the table, "why don't you tell me what's wrong."

"It's Dotty," she whispered, almost in tears. "We can't find anything for her to eat! We went to the shop and the woman said..."

Tara broke off, too upset to continue.

Professor P looked at us puzzled. "Dotty?" he said confused. "Your iguana?"

"Dotty's not an iguana," I said. "She's a dinosaur, a real living dinosaur."

"A dinosaur!" Professor P said, taken aback. "But they're extinct."

"That's what we thought," I said. "But we checked on Tara's computer. Dotty really is a diplodocus."

Professor P looked baffled. "I think you'd better start at the beginning," he said.

Tara took a deep breath and began.

"A few days ago a parcel arrived at my house," she said. "Inside was an egg. We thought it was a plastic dinosaur egg that Mary had sent us for our exhibition."

"But it wasn't plastic," I added. "It was a real egg. And Dotty came out. Mary thought Dotty might be a type of lizard called an iguana."

"So I went to the pet shop," Tara explained, "to get some things for Dotty. But she didn't look like any of the lizards in the book I bought. And she wouldn't eat anything either."

As Tara paused for breath, I continued, "That's when we checked on Tara's computer. It scanned Dotty and said she's a diplodocus."

"A diplodocus!" Professor P exclaimed. "Are you sure?"

"The computer was a hundred percent certain," I replied. "And it said that baby diplodocus need to eat cycadeoid plants. So we went to the plant shop..."

"And they're extinct!" Tara burst out. "There's nothing for her to eat. What are we going to do, Professor P? Dotty will die if we don't find her something to eat soon!"

As we were talking, I noticed Floppy was unusually quiet and looked rather uncomfortable.

Suddenly he cried out, "It's not my fault!"

"Nobody said it was, Floppy," Professor P said, slightly taken aback by his unexpected outburst.

Floppy chewed his ears and looked down guiltily. Professor P peered at him closely.

"What do you know about this, Floppy?" Professor P asked sternly.

"I thought Tara would be pleased," Floppy said meekly. "I didn't mean any harm."

"I think you'd better explain..." Professor P began.

"I ordered the egg for Tara," Floppy admitted sheepishly.

"You ordered it?" Professor P said puzzled. "Where from?"

"From the Intergalactic Web," Floppy replied. "When we first logged onto the IGW, I discovered a dinosaur website where you could buy all kinds of dinosaur things. It was amazing, Professor P!"

"Really!" Professor P said, fascinated.

"And on the website they were giving away a mystery gift!" Floppy continued. "Well, I remembered Peter and

Tara were making a dinosaur exhibition, so I ordered it for Tara."

"But how did it get to my house?" Tara asked, bewildered.

"The aliens teleported it," Floppy replied.

"Astonishing!" Professor P exclaimed. "They teleported it through space! What technology!"

"I didn't know what the gift was," Floppy continued, "and I never guessed it would be a real dinosaur egg. I didn't know what would happen! I'm sorry, Tara."

"It wasn't your fault, Floppy," Tara said softly. "But what are we going to do now? Dotty can't last much longer without food."

"If we could get back onto the IGW," Professor P said thoughtfully, "we could probably order some food for Dotty. But with the QED chip blown up..."

Professor P fell silent.

Suddenly Floppy turned into an owl and flew round the room excitedly.

"I've got it!" he cried. "I know what we can do!"

Tara and I looked at him expectantly.

"We can use the IDP!" Floppy continued.

"The IDP?" we repeated, confused.

"What do think, Professor P?" Floppy asked. "Is it possible?"

Professor P stroked his beard thoughtfully. "Yes, possible," he said, "but dangerous. There are still bugs to iron out..."

"We've got to try, Professor P," Floppy exclaimed, "or Dotty will die!"

"All right!" Professor P said, standing up suddenly. "There's no time to lose. I'll get everything ready. Peter, Tara, go home and wait for me, I'll pick you up as soon as I can. We'll be gone a few hours so wrap up well."

"And don't forget to bring Dotty," Floppy added.

I looked at Tara in astonishment.

"But...what...why?" I stammered.

"What are we going to do, Professor P?" Tara asked, perplexed.

"You'll see," he replied mysteriously.

CHAPTER THIRTEEN

Rough Ride

As we rushed down the lane, we chatted excitedly about our visit to Professor P.

"Oh, I'm really glad we went to see Professor P," Tara said happily. "I knew he'll be able to get some food for Dotty!"

"I still can't believe she came from outer space!" I said in astonishment.

Tara nodded. "It doesn't seem possible, does it? Aliens, other worlds, the Intergalactic Web! But Dotty's real enough!"

"She must have been teleported millions of miles through space!" I said, "from some place where they breed dinosaurs! A dinosaur planet!"

"I guess there must be planets out there where dinosaurs never died out, like they did here on earth," Tara added thoughtfully,

"Well, it's a good thing Floppy didn't order a T-Rex!" I chuckled. "I wouldn't want one of those for a pet!"

"No way!" Tara laughed.

When we reached the main road, I put Sparky on the lead and we ran the rest of the way home. When we arrived at Tara's house, we went straight up to Rosie's room. Rosie had made a large playpen for Dotty out of wooden building bricks and filled it with dinosaur toys.

"Hi, Rosie," Tara greeted her, "Is Dotty all right?"

"She tried to eat Dippy!" Rosie replied crossly.

Tara knelt down beside Dotty and picked her up. The little dinosaur nibbled her hand gently.

"I know you're hungry," Tara said kindly, "but don't worry, Professor P will be here soon. He's going to find some food for you."

"Eeek! Eeek!" Dotty cried. She looked up at Tara and seemed to understand.

"We'll need to keep Dotty warm on the journey, Tara," I said thoughtfully.

"I'll see what I can find," Tara said, standing up.

Tara left the room and returned a few moments later with a cardboard box and a pink fluffy towel. She lined the cardboard box with the towel and laid Dotty inside. The little creature curled up and promptly went to sleep.

"She's exhausted," Tara said softly.

"Night, night, Dotty," Rosie added as she wrapped the towel around Dotty.

Tara poked some holes in the lid and fitted it onto the box. Then she stuck down the lid with sticky tape to make it secure.

"She'll be fine now," Tara said, pleased.

We left Rosie playing in her room and carried the box downstairs. Tara put the box into her rucksack and left it by the door.

"I wonder when Professor P will get here," Tara said, glancing at her watch. "Do you want something to eat while we're waiting, Peter?"

"Yes, thanks, I'm starving," I replied. "It's ages since I had breakfast!"

We went into the kitchen to have a snack and I gave Sparky some dog biscuits. We had just finished eating when the doorbell rang. We rushed excitedly to the front door, hoping it was Professor P.

"Hi, Professor P!" we greeted him happily.

"Ready?" Professor P asked with a smile. We nodded excitedly.

"I'll just get Dotty," Tara said, grabbing her rucksack.

Tara, Sparky and I ran over to Professor P's open-top car. Brains was sitting in the passenger seat with Floppy perched on his shoulder. He looked like an owl and was wearing a pair of large, ridiculous looking goggles. Sleepy was sitting in the back, resting her paws on the driver's seat.

Tara and I climbed into the back seat and Sparky jumped onto my lap. Sleepy sat between us and wagged her tail excitedly.

"Let's go!" Professor P said as he started the engine.

"Where are we going, Professor P?" I asked eagerly.

"You'll see," he replied mysteriously.

I looked at Tara puzzled. We still had no idea where Professor P was taking us!

"Hold on!" Floppy cried as the car shot forward.

I hugged Sparky tightly to my chest as we sped down the road. As we raced down the hill, the wind rushed by so fast I could hardly breathe. Sleepy's ears flapped in the wind and she barked in excitement.

A few minutes later, we arrived at the beach car park and skidded to a halt at the far end, by the steps leading down onto the beach.

I looked at Tara in surprise. Why had Professor P taken us to the beach?

"Professor P," I said as I started to get out of the car, "What are we doing…?"

"Don't get out yet, Peter," Professor P said, with a twinkle in his eye. "Our journey is only just beginning!"

"You just wait!" Floppy added knowingly.

Professor P reached over to the dashboard and slid back a small panel to reveal a big red button.

"Get ready for the ride of your life!" Floppy exclaimed as Professor P pressed the button.

Nothing happened. Professor P pressed it again. Still nothing happened. I looked at Tara puzzled.

"Oh, black holes!" Professor P muttered. "It must have jammed!"

"We'll fix it!" Floppy cried, eager to help. "Come on, Brains!"

Brains jumped out of the car and raised the bonnet with one hand. Floppy changed into oil stained overalls and peered into the engine compartment. He nodded confidently. Tara looked at me and giggled.

"Yes, I can see the problem," Floppy said. "We need to free up the rubber skirt – it's caught on the wheels. Brains, get a hammer, please."

Brains took a huge hammer out of the tool case at the rear of the car.

"Is this one big enough?" he asked as he effortlessly raised it above his head.

"Careful!" Professor P cried. "Don't harm the..."

"All under control, Professor P," Floppy interrupted. "Now, Brains, you need to hit just here. But gently!"

Brains lowered the hammer and swung it carefully.

Bang!

"Well done, Brains," Floppy said, "one more time, for luck."

Brains raised the hammer again.

Bang! Clunk!

"That should do it," Floppy said as he and Brains got back into the car. "It should work fine now, Professor P."

"I hope so," Professor P replied, not quite so sure.

Professor P pressed the red button on the dashboard again. This time a loud clanging sound rang out from around the outside of the car. I leaned out to see what had caused it. A large black rubber skirt now covered the bottom part of the car.

"You did it, Brains," Professor P said, delighted.

As Professor P pulled back the steering wheel, a loud whooshing sound burst out from under the car. Sand blew in all directions and the car began to hover just above the ground.

"A hovercraft!" I said in amazement.

"Hold on tightly!" Professor P shouted.

A deafening roar filled the air and the car shot forward. It flew over the steps and landed on the beach at speed, throwing us forward with a sudden jolt. Sparky barked in alarm and I had to hold onto him tightly to stop him from jumping out.

The hovercraft accelerated. It flew faster and faster across the beach. We soon reached the sea and hurtled into the waves. Spray flew up into the air. I was dripping wet!

"Weee, this is fun!" Floppy cried as he turned into a dolphin and pretended to dive in and out of the waves.

Fun? I was wet and cold from the icy sea spray! But what an adventure! This was why I loved being with Professor P and Floppy – you never knew what was going to happen next!

"Where are we going, Professor P?" Tara shouted, trying to make herself heard above the noise of the engine.

"Soon be there!" Professor P yelled in reply.

Tara prodded my arm.

"Look, Peter! I think we're going to the island!" she said excitedly.

It was true, we were turning towards the island. This was very strange – why was Professor P taking us there? What was on the island that would help get Dotty some food?

As we headed out to sea, the wind picked up and the car was thrown back and forth by the waves. Through the spray, I could see the island approaching. Rocks surrounded most of the island and the only safe place to land was a small sandy cove on the right.

"Nearly there!" Professor P said as he steered us towards the cove.

We were about fifty metres from the island when a huge wave crashed into the car. It completely soaked us. The engine coughed, spluttered and then died. Professor P turned the key in the ignition. The engine started briefly and then cut out again.

"Most unfortunate," Professor P said, trying to sound calm.

"What are we going to do, Professor P?" Brains cried in panic. "I can't swim! I can only sink!"

Tara and I were both good swimmers. We could easily have reached the island on a calm summer day. But today, on a freezing morning, we would never make it in the icy cold waves.

"We could paddle," I suggested. "It's not far."

"Good idea, Peter," Professor P agreed.

We all leant over the side and paddled as best we could.

"Not so hard, Brains!" Professor P warned. "You're making us go round in circles!"

"Sorry, Professor P," Brains apologised.

We soon got into a rhythm and began to make progress towards the island.

We had almost reached the cove when bubbles began rising up from underneath the car. The right side of the car was dipping down into the water.

"We're sinking!" I cried in dismay.

"We're doomed!" Brains said, covering his face with his hand.

"We're not going to make it, Professor P!" Tara said as she bailed out the water.

"Hold on!" Professor P said. "I'll give the engine another try."

He turned the ignition key. The engine coughed. Then it roared into life. I breathed a sigh of relief.

"That's more like it!" Professor P cried as the car rose up out of the water again.

Moments later, we reached the cove. Professor P stopped the car at the end of the beach. He pressed the red button on the dashboard and the rubber skirt on the underside of the car retracted.

I opened the car door to get out.

"Hang on, Peter," Professor P said. "We're not there, yet."

I looked at Tara puzzled.

"Where are we going, then?" I asked as I shut the door.

"You'll see in a moment," Professor P replied, mysteriously.

He started the engine and drove carefully along a narrow grassy path through the woods.

"Mind the branches," he said as we squeezed between two large trees.

Finally, we drove out of the woods and into a large clearing. Professor P stopped the car.

"We're here," he announced.

Tara and I gasped in amazement as we stared at a huge structure in the centre of the clearing.

Hanging from a metal scaffolding were three sparkling yellow tubes in the shape of a triangle. I could hear a strange humming sound coming from the structure and an unpleasant smell like burnt plastic filled the air.

I looked at Tara, bewildered. What was this strange device? And how was it going to help us get food for Dotty?

CHAPTER FOURTEEN

The IDP

Professor P jumped out of the car and strode over to the huge structure. Tara, Sparky and I quickly followed him.

An enormous metal scaffolding towered above us. Attached to it with shiny steel wires were three thick tubes in the shape of a triangle. Inside the tubes, I could see a sparkling yellow liquid. Thick red, green and black wires led from the tubes to a large grey box to the right of the scaffolding.

At the base of the triangle was a low wooden ramp. Sparky walked onto the ramp and sniffed at the structure warily, the hair on his back standing up. I noticed a strange burning smell and a faint crackling sound coming from the tubes. A warning sign on the scaffolding read, *Danger High Voltage!*

"What is it, Professor P?" I asked.

Before he could reply, Floppy burst out, "Standing before you is the IDP! The Inter Dimensional Portal! The most amazing and utterly outstanding invention in the world!"

"The what?" I asked, confused.

"The IDP is a doorway to another world!" Professor P explained, his eyes shining with excitement. "It can take you to anywhere in the universe..."

"Anywhere and any-when!" Floppy interrupted, flapping around the structure excitedly.

I looked at Tara in astonishment. So this was the mysterious invention Professor P had been working on!

"A time machine!" Tara exclaimed incredulously.

"It's better than a time machine!" Professor P explained proudly. "With an ordinary time machine you can easily end up coming back to a different time or place. But the IDP has no such problems!"

"But how…" I began.

I was bursting with questions. How did it work? Why had Professor P build it? Why was it on the island? Was it safe?

"I'll explain everything shortly, Peter," Professor P chuckled. "First I need to get the IDP set up. I haven't had a chance to test it with such a large time difference but I believe I can get it to open in the Jurassic…"

"The Jurassic!" I exclaimed.

"So we can get some food for Dotty?" Tara added excitedly.

"That's the plan!" Professor P replied. "I'm going to set the portal to open in the late Jurassic Period, in Colorado, America. Plenty of diplodocus fossils have been found there, so with luck, we should be able to find the right kind of food for Dotty."

"Oh, that's brilliant!" Tara cried, delighted. "I'll go and tell Dotty!"

Tara dashed back to the car. I stayed with Professor P as he bent down beside the grey control box and opened it. Inside the box was a notebook computer resting on a tangle of coloured wires and four large car batteries.

I watched in fascination as Professor P opened the computer and began typing at the keyboard. I could hardly believe what was about to happen! Would the portal really work? Would we actually be able to go back to the world of the dinosaurs?

Tara came over a few minutes later. "Dotty's still asleep," she said cheerfully. "How's it going, Professor P?"

"Finished," he replied, confidently. "I've just started the power up sequence. The portal should open in a few minutes."

"We'd better take cover," Floppy said as he flew over to the car. "It makes quite a bang."

I took a firm hold of Sparky's collar and quickly led him over to the car. We all crouched down behind the car and waited excitedly. Sleepy lay trustingly at Professor P's feet. Floppy perched on Professor P's shoulder and covered his eyes with his wings.

"I don't like loud bangs," Brains moaned as he put his fingers in his ears.

Suddenly a crackling noise like the sound of fireworks filled the air. I looked round the side of the car to see what was happening. The tubes were flashing and sparks were flying everywhere! I felt quite dizzy looking at it!

"Look away, Peter!" Professor P warned.

I turned my gaze and as I did, an enormous explosion shook the island. It was the loudest noise I had ever heard! Along with the noise, a flash of brilliant yellow light lit up the island and I felt a blast of heat hit my face. Then everything became still. Sparky pressed against me and I could feel him shaking – he was terrified, too scared even to bark.

"Slightly louder than I expected," Professor P apologised. "Is everybody all right?"

Tara and I nodded. Sleepy barked. Sparky made a whimpering sound and nuzzled against me.

Brains took his fingers out of his ears. "My head hurts!" he said, trying to stand up. He wobbled unsteadily and looked very dizzy.

"Let's see if it worked!" Floppy cried excitedly, flying back towards the portal.

Professor P stood up and strode after him. Tara and I followed. I looked at the portal closely. The tubes were glowing steadily. Before the explosion, I could see through the hollow triangle to the trees beyond – but now a silver grey mist filled the space and blocked the view. As I peered into the shimmering mist, I could just make out patterns of light and shadowy figures moving in the distance.

Professor P opened the grey control box and examined the notebook computer screen.

"I believe it has worked!" he said delightedly. "We have successfully linked to the Jurassic, 156 million years in the past!"

"So we can get some food for Dotty, then?" Tara asked eagerly.

"Yes," Professor P replied, "but first we need to make sure it's working correctly. We need someone to go through the portal and make sure it's safe."

He looked questioningly at Brains. Brains was swaying unsteadily from side to side, obviously still dizzy from the explosion.

"It has to be someone big and strong and not afraid of danger," Floppy joined in, winking at Professor P. "Now, who could possibly go?"

Floppy stroked his chin and looked thoughtful. Brains stroked his chin and tried to look thoughtful too.

"We need a hero!" Professor P said dramatically. "A hero to boldly go back in time! Perhaps someone made of metal…"

Brains suddenly burst out. "I can do it! I'm big and strong and brave and made of metal. Can I go, please, Professor P?"

"Of course, Brains!" Professor P said, smiling. "You're perfect for the job!"

Brains strode towards the portal.

"But not yet, Brains!" Professor P called out. "I need to tell you what to do, first."

"Our hero fails at the first hurdle," Floppy muttered.

"Now, Brains, I want you to go through the portal," Professor P said, "look around briefly, then come straight back and tell us what you saw."

"OK," Brains said thoughtfully. "Go through, come back." He paused, "What was the bit in the middle, Professor P?"

Tara and I giggled as Professor P replied, "Look around, Brains. Don't wander off, will you?"

"Go through, look around, don't wander off…" Brains repeated, scratching his head. "And there was something else? That's four things to remember. I can only remember three things at the same time."

"Lucky if he remembers three!" Floppy quipped.

"Go through, look around, come back," Professor P repeated patiently.

"OK, got it," Brains said as he walked towards the portal.

"Good luck, Brains!" I called out.

When Brains reached the glowing tubes, he cautiously put out his hand to touch the silvery mist. His arm passed through and disappeared. He pulled his hand back and looked at it. He moved his fingers and nodded, satisfied that they were unharmed. Then he stepped into the mist and disappeared.

"I hope he'll be OK," Tara said looking concerned.

We waited nervously, staring at the portal. A few minutes passed and Brains did not return. Floppy flew around the portal, trying to peer inside.

"He should be back by now," Professor P said, glancing at his watch.

"Do you think he's all right, Professor P?" I asked anxiously.

"I'm not sure," Professor P replied. "The portal may have disrupted his electronics. I shall have to go through and find him."

I glanced worriedly at Tara.

"Are you sure that's safe, Professor P?" she asked.

"I'm sure the portal is working correctly," he replied confidently, "but Brains might not be. Don't worry, I'll come straight back if there's any sign of danger."

"Be careful, Professor P!" Floppy cried out.

Professor P went over to the portal. Sleepy ran to his side and looked up at him expectantly.

"Wait here, Sleepy," Professor P said, gently stroking her head. "It might be dangerous."

Professor P reached out his hand towards the portal. He pulled it back sharply when it touched the silvery mist.

"Are you all right, Professor P?" I asked.

"Just a slight tingling," he replied, "like a mild electric shock, nothing to worry about."

I watched with bated breath as Professor P took a step forward. He was just about to enter the mist when Brains suddenly burst through the portal!

Brains collided with Professor P, knocking him to the ground. Then he tripped over Professor P and landed with a loud clatter on the ground.

"Thank goodness you're back, Brains!" Professor P said as he stood up and dusted himself off.

Brains rose slowly to his feet. "I did it!" he said proudly. "I'm a hero!"

"Well done, Brains," we congratulated him.

"Why were you so long, Brains?" Floppy asked. "We were really worried."

"I wasn't long!" Brains protested. "I did just what Professor P said. I went through, looked around and came back!"

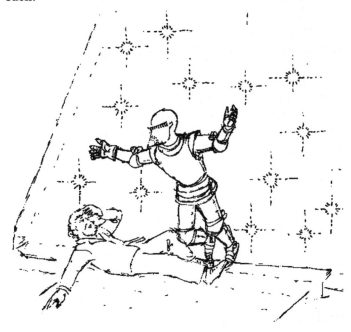

"Strange," Professor P mused, "There must be a slight time discontinuity, perhaps due to the uncertainty…"

"Oh, I forgot," Brains added. "I did walk off. Then I got a bit lost."

"Typical," Floppy sighed.

Tara glanced at me and giggled.

"What did you see, Brains?" Professor P asked eagerly.

"Dinosaurs!" Brains replied. "Big dinosaurs! Lots of them!"

"What did they look like?" I asked excitedly.

We did not hear what Brains said next as his voice was drowned out by a loud roar from behind us. I turned and froze in terror. A huge dinosaur with red markings above its eyes and green stripes on its tail was standing in the centre of the clearing.

It opened its mouth and I stared in horror at the rows of sharp serrated teeth!

"Run!" Floppy cried out. "Run for your lives!"

CHAPTER FIFTEEN

Allosaurus Attack

I stared in terror at the huge dinosaur towering above us. It stood on two powerful hind legs and glared down at us menacingly. Three sharp claws glistened in the sunlight on each of its front legs.

There was a look of confusion in its eyes. It was obviously unsure about this cold world with its strange and unfamiliar smells. It glanced around warily.

"Nobody move!" Professor P said in a quiet commanding voice. "It won't be able to see us so clearly if we stay absolutely still."

"What are we going to do, Professor P?" Tara asked, her voice shaking.

"Don't worry," Professor P reassured us, "we're going to be all right. I have some things in the car that will protect us."

I glanced over towards the car. It was about ten metres away. Sparky and Sleepy were waiting by the side of the car, crouching down low, eyeing the dinosaur. Unfortunately, the huge creature was blocking the way to the car.

"We'll walk slowly to the trees behind us," Professor P whispered, "then make our way over to the car through the woods."

"OK," I said nervously, taking a small step backwards.

"Not yet, Peter," Professor P warned. "First, we need a diversion. Brains, I want you to distract the dinosaur while we go over to the car."

"Distract it?" Brains repeated, unsure. "But…It's very big, Professor P."

"We really need your help, Brains," Professor P urged. "I know you can do it!"

"You'll be our hero!" Tara added encouragingly.

"All right," Brains said and strode bravely towards the dinosaur.

After taking a few steps, he stopped abruptly, turned and came back.

"How do I distract it, Professor P?" he asked puzzled.

"I'll help!" Floppy said boldly, turning into a pterodactyl and flying round in circles. "Come on, Brains, let's go!"

"Good luck," Professor P said as he clipped Floppy's sphere to Brains's shoulder.

I watched anxiously as Brains began to walk toward the dinosaur. It stared at him threateningly.

"It's very big, Floppy," Brains said, looking up at the huge creature. "And it has sharp teeth. Lots of them!"

"Keep going, Brains," Floppy urged. "You can do it!"

Brains stopped a few metres from the dinosaur and waved his hands in the air.

"Shoo," he said tentatively. "Go away, dinosaur!"

The huge dinosaur glared down at him. Sunlight reflected off Brains into the dinosaur's eyes. It squinted at the shiny suit of armour, obviously unsure what it was.

"Yes, you, dinosaur," Brains said more confidently. "I'm talking to you!"

The dinosaur took a step towards Brains, lowered its head and let out a blood-curdling roar. I jumped in terror. Tara screamed.

"It's not a friendly dinosaur, Floppy," Brains wailed as he staggered away from the dinosaur. "Not at all friendly!"

"Wait here, Brains," Floppy said firmly. "I'll see what I can do."

With a pop, Floppy turned into a large plump dinosaur, with bright orange triangular plates running down its back. Apart from the floppy ears, he was a perfect imitation of a stegosaurus.

"Hey, dinosaur," Floppy called as he slowly waddled towards the portal. "Over here!"

The dinosaur eyed the stegosaurus hungrily. This was the first familiar creature it had seen since coming through the portal.

"Why don't you come and eat me?" Floppy added teasingly.

The dinosaur walked slowly towards Floppy, getting ready to pounce. Floppy walked quickly towards the portal. I watched anxiously as the dinosaur followed him, hoping the plan would work.

Professor P whispered to us. "Peter, Tara, let's go over to the woods now."

Slowly, we walked backwards towards the trees, being careful not to make any sudden movement that might distract the dinosaur. When we finally reached the cover of the woods, I let out a sigh of relief.

Floppy had now reached the portal and was pretending to go through it. The dinosaur slowed as it reached the portal and looked nervously at the strange shimmering mist. It tentatively took a step forwards and then stopped, unwilling to go any further.

Floppy was almost through when the dinosaur finally decided to act. It pounced like lightning on Floppy's tail, biting down with its full force. I heard a loud crack as its teeth passed straight though Floppy.

The dinosaur howled in pain. Blood trickled from its mouth. It jumped away from the portal, stunned and confused. It dabbed at its mouth with its front claw and then glanced around, looking for somewhere to lick its wounds.

I watched in horror as it saw the woods and came straight towards us! It would find us in a moment!

"Floppy! Do something!" Professor P called out, urgently.

Suddenly an even larger dinosaur appeared! It was Floppy – he had changed into a very impressive T-rex! He stood blocking the path between the dinosaur and us. Floppy raised himself up and made a terrifying roar.

The dinosaur roared back. Floppy roared even louder. The two enormous creatures stood glaring at each other. It was a stand off.

"Follow me! Now!" Professor P ordered as he led the way through the woods.

I could hardly keep up with Professor P. I stumbled through the sharp brambles that were tearing at my clothes. I glanced behind and saw Tara struggling to keep up, her face pale with fear.

A few moments later, Professor P stopped and raised his hand.

"Wait here!" he whispered. "We're as close as we can get. I'll run to the car and get the box of dino defences. Don't leave the safety of the woods under any circumstances! I'll be back in a moment."

Tara and I watched anxiously as Professor P stepped cautiously out into the clearing.

I heard a sudden loud roar. I turned and saw the dinosaur lunge at Floppy. It lashed out with its front claw but it passed straight through Floppy. The dinosaur lost its balance and fell to the ground with a thud.

The dinosaur awkwardly got back on its feet. Now, it looked even more mean and angry than before. It ran straight through Floppy, roaring in frustration and annoyance.

The dinosaur turned and saw Professor P, completely exposed, halfway between the woods and the car. A few giant strides of its powerful hind legs and it reached him. Tara screamed in horror. Terrified, I held my breath as the dinosaur lowered it head. It bared its teeth and I could smell its foul stale breath.

"Woof! Woof!" Sleepy barked madly.

She dashed over and placed herself between the dinosaur and Professor P. It turned and swiped at her with its front claws. She moved just in time as the sharp claws narrowly missed her. She jumped up and then ran off, trying to lead the dinosaur away from Professor P.

It worked! The dinosaur went after Sleepy. Professor P ran to the car. I watched tensely as he opened the boot of the car and took out a large metal box.

"That must be the dino defences," I said to Tara, relieved.

"Thank goodness!" she cried.

I heard a loud yelp. Sleepy was on the ground, hurt. The dinosaur lunged at her! She sprang to her feet just in time. But she was limping. Her front leg was bleeding. The dinosaur was gaining on her!

Suddenly Sparky run out from under the car and raced towards the dinosaur, barking madly

"No, Sparky," I cried, horrified.

I watched in horror as the angry dinosaur rounded on Sparky. What chance could he possibly have against such a huge creature? He was only a puppy.

"Brains, do something!" Professor P called out in desperation as he fumbled with the lock on the metal box.

Floppy turned into a pterodactyl again and flew over to Brains who was standing by the portal, unsure what to do.

"Follow me, Brains," Floppy cried as he flew towards the woods. "Quick!"

Brains raced over to trees as fast as he could.

"Pick that up!" Floppy ordered, pointing to a huge fallen tree trunk.

Brains bent down and raised the tree trunk above his head.

"Now, hit that dinosaur!" Floppy cried.

Brains ran wildly towards the dinosaur. As the dinosaur turned to defend itself, Sparky ran for cover. I breathed a sigh of relief. Sparky was safe at last!

"Take that!" Brains said forcefully, ramming the tree trunk into the dinosaur's leg.

The dinosaur roared in anger and staggered away obviously hurt and frightened.

"I did it!" Brains cried triumphantly.

He raised the tree trunk again and marched purposely towards the dinosaur. Unfortunately, he did not get far. He tripped and fell to the ground with a clatter.

While Brains was getting to his feet, the dinosaur turned back to the dogs. They ran away blindly as the huge creature lumbered towards them. I watched in dismay as I realised where they were going. They were heading straight towards the portal!

"Sparky, Sleepy! No! Come back!" I cried out in desperation.

But it was too late. The dogs ran straight into the triangle and disappeared into the silver mist. The dinosaur stopped abruptly and looked around confused, wondering where the dogs had gone.

Brains had picked himself up from the ground and saw his chance. He ran towards the dinosaur, his armour clattering, tree trunk raised high above his head. He was a fearsome sight. The dinosaur saw him and fled through the portal after the dogs.

Brains skidded to a halt in front of the portal. He looked over towards Professor P, unsure whether to follow.

Tara and I ran out of the woods and over to Professor P.

"What are we going to do, Professor P?" I exclaimed in dismay. "Sleepy and Sparky! They've gone through the portal!"

"And the dinosaur is after them!" Tara cried.

"We've got to rescue them!" Professor P replied immediately. "Brains, Floppy, go through the portal. Find Sleepy and Sparky!"

Without hesitation, Brains and Floppy dived through the portal.

"Peter, Tara, get in the car!" Professor P ordered. "We're going through too!"

Tara and I jumped into the back seat. Professor P threw the *Dino Defences* box onto the seat with us and started the engine. It burst into life and Professor P slammed the car into gear.

"Hold on tight!" he cried as we hurtled towards the portal.

CHAPTER SIXTEEN

Dino Defences

As we entered the portal, I was blinded by a brilliant flash of light. For a moment, time seemed to stand still and I felt as though I was floating in a sea of sparkling yellow light. Then the car burst through the portal and we landed with a jolt on the other side.

Professor P slammed on the brakes and we came to an abrupt halt.

"Everyone all right?" he asked, turning round to check.

"I'm OK," Tara replied, brushing the hair away from her face.

"Just a bit dizzy," I said, rubbing the bump on my head.

The dizzy feeling soon passed and I looked around curiously, squinting in the bright sunshine. It was all so different from the world we had left. We were on a plain, covered in small bushes and scattered trees. In the far distance, I could see hills covered in forest. Strange unfamiliar smells filled the air and it was burning hot.

"Look, Peter," Tara said excitedly, pointing overhead.

I felt a surge of excitement as I saw a huge pterodactyl soaring above us! We really were millions of years in the past, back in the age of the dinosaurs!

"No sign of that dinosaur," Professor P said looking around warily.

"Or Brains and Floppy," Tara added.

I scoured the landscape for them or of any sign of Sleepy and Sparky. Then, out of the corner of my eye, I saw a flash of light. It was Brains, running through the trees with Floppy flying overhead.

"Over there, Professor P!" I cried, pointing to the woods on our left.

"Hold on!" Professor P said as he slammed the car into gear and accelerated towards the trees.

The car shook unsteadily as we sped across the bumpy ground.

"Toot! Toot!" Professor P sounded the horn as we approached Brains and Floppy.

They saw us and ran over to the car. Professor P braked hard and we skidded to a halt.

"We lost them!" Floppy cried unhappily, as he flew over. "We couldn't keep up! They were too fast!"

"Where did they go?" Professor P asked anxiously.

"Through those trees," Floppy answered.

"Quick, get in the car, Brains," Professor P said firmly.

Brains jumped into the front seat and the car shot forwards again. Professor P wove the car through the trees and in a few moments, we were out of the woods on a hill. The ground in front sloped down towards a small lake surrounded by palm trees.

"Which way now, Floppy?" Professor P asked urgently.

"That way," Floppy cried, "towards the lake."

Professor P accelerated the car down the slope. I held on tightly to the front seat as the car bounced over the uneven ground.

"The dogs are probably hiding in those trees there," Professor P said, as we approached the lake.

I looked anxiously for any sign of Sleepy and Sparky. Beside the lake was a jungle of palm trees, creepers and smaller bushes. It was a great place for the dogs to hide.

Professor P slowed the car as we reached the lake and tooted the horn.

"Sparky, where are you?" I called out desperately.

But there was no friendly bark in reply. Instead, I heard a loud and terrifying roar. A huge dinosaur sprang out from the trees and stood directly in front of us. It looked like the same dinosaur as before but even fiercer.

"Oh, no!" I cried as I saw the bright red blood dripping from its mouth. Surely, it wasn't from Sleepy or Sparky!

Professor P slammed on the brakes and wrenched the steering wheel round to the left. We skidded around in a circle and stopped with the back of the car now just metres from the dinosaur.

Professor P stamped his foot down on the accelerator. The wheels spun, sending a cloud of dust into the face of the dinosaur as we sped away. The dinosaur snorted angrily and then followed us as we drove back the way we had come. It was keeping pace, just metres behind, waiting for the chance to strike.

"Peter, Tara, get the Dino Defences!" Professor P ordered.

I grabbed the box from under the seat. Tara and I fumbled with the catch on the box as the car bumped over the rough ground. We managed to wrench the box open. Inside was a strange assortment of objects – coloured cylinders, cones and spheres.

"What do we do, Professor P?" I cried anxiously.

"Look for a torch," Professor P replied.

"I've got it," I said, picking up a small black torch. But it was no ordinary torch – it had a small black loudspeaker in place of the bulb.

"It's a sonic torch," Professor P explained. "It gives out ultrasonic pulses that repel most animals. Switch it on and point it at the dinosaur."

I pressed the on switch and it gave out a loud whining sound. I turned round and pointed the torch at the dinosaur. Nothing happened.

"It's not working, Professor P," I cried as the dinosaur continued to keep pace with the car.

"Turn the knob on the side," Professor P said. "When you get the right frequency it will scare the dinosaur away."

I turned the knob and the whining sound got higher in pitch. Finally, it became too high for me to hear. The dinosaur could obviously hear it though. It roared and shook its head in distress.

"It's working!" Tara cried delighted.

The dinosaur slowed its pace and then stopped. It turned its head to one side and struck at its ear with its front claw.

"Look out!" Floppy cried. "Over there!"

Another huge dinosaur had come out of the jungle and was racing towards us. It effortlessly overtook the car and blocked our path. Professor P slammed on the brakes and we skidded to a halt.

I pointed my sonic torch at the dinosaur. It stopped and roared angrily. I glanced behind. The other dinosaur was closing in!

"Tara, get the other sonic torch," Professor P said firmly.

Tara grabbed the torch from the box and pointed it at the dinosaur behind us. I kept my sonic torch trained on the dinosaur in front. We were holding them at bay!

But then another dinosaur appeared, approaching from the side. We were surrounded!

"We can't hold them all off!" Tara cried, desperately waving her sonic torch at them wildly. "They're closing in!"

"Peter, pass me your sonic torch," Professor P said.

I gave it to him and he pointed it at the dinosaur in front of the car.

"Look in the box for some coloured balls," he continued.

I reached into the Dino Defences box and took out a clear blue plastic ball, about the size of a plum. Inside the ball, I could see a small electronic circuit and tiny battery.

"I found one, Professor P," I said.

"Good, now throw it at the feet of the dinosaur," Professor P ordered.

I hurled the ball towards the dinosaur that was approaching us from the side. It hit the ground and let out a flash of blue light. Then it rocketed upwards at twice the speed and let out a loud screech. The ball smashed into the side of the dinosaur, bounced off and continued bouncing around, letting out a fearsome sound and sending out bright flashes of light.

The dinosaur jumped back and roared in surprise. It lashed out at the ball, missed and almost lost its balance. The other dinosaurs looked on warily, unsure about the strange object.

"It's working!" Floppy cried out as they began to retreat.

The ball bounced off the ground and flew straight towards the dinosaur's head. It reacted instantly, swatting the ball with its front arm and sending it flying into a tree. The ball smashed to pieces. I watched as it fell to the ground, broken.

"Quickly, throw some more!" Floppy urged.

Tara put her torch down and we scooped up a handful of the coloured balls. We threw them at the dinosaurs as hard as we could. It was mayhem! The balls hit the dinosaurs, fell to the ground and then bounced back even faster. With each bounce, they gained in energy, bouncing higher and higher.

The dinosaurs cried out as the balls screeched and flashed all around them. They looked absolutely terrified! They turned and ran in terror, not looking backwards.

"They've gone!" I sighed in relief as I slumped back into the car seat.

"No time to rest, Peter!" Professor P said firmly. "Everyone get out of the car. We must collect the balls before they get lost – we may need them again if the dinosaurs return. Floppy, you keep watch."

"Aye, aye, captain," Floppy said, putting a long telescope to his eye.

Tara and I jumped out of the car and ran into the midst of the bouncing balls. Brains walked slowly and cautiously towards them.

"Hurry, Brains," Professor P urged. "The dinosaurs may return any minute!"

Brains glanced around anxiously. Then he ran towards the balls, arms outstretched, and tried to catch one. He looked very confused as the balls bounced off him with loud clanging noises.

We all desperately raced around trying to catch the balls. It was hard work in the heat but eventually we managed to collect them all. When all the balls were safely in the box, Tara and I sat down beside the car, exhausted. Professor P gave us both a bottle of water and I eagerly took a drink.

As I put the bottle down, I heard the sound of barking. I looked up and saw Sparky and Sleepy bounding towards us. I ran over to them and gave Sparky a big hug. He wagged his tail so hard I thought it would fall off.

"Thank goodness you're all right, Sparky!" I cried. I had never been so pleased to see him!

"And Sleepy's fine too!" Professor P said happily, as he bent down to examine her. "She's only got a slight graze!"

Professor P poured some water into a bowl for the dogs and they lapped it up eagerly.

"Well, at last we're all together again," Professor P said, when the dogs had finished, "but I don't want to risk those dinosaurs returning. I think I'd better move the car to a safer place. We're very exposed here."

We all got back into the car. Professor P drove to the top of a small hill and stopped in the shade of a group of palm trees.

"This should be fine," he said, getting out of the car. "We have a good view in all directions. Keep a look out for dinosaurs, Floppy!"

"OK, Professor P," Floppy said, turning into a huge pterodactyl and flying up to the top one of the palm trees.

I got out of the car and looked around. Now we were all safely together again, our Jurassic adventure could begin!

CHAPTER SEVENTEEN

Jurassic Journey

Tara grabbed her rucksack and got out of the car.

"I hope Dotty wasn't too frightened by those dinosaurs," she said, opening the rucksack.

She took out the cardboard box and gently picked up Dotty.

"Eek, eek!" the little creature cried and nuzzled Tara affectionately.

"So this is your dinosaur, Tara!" Professor P said, looking at Dotty in amazement.

"Yes, do you want to hold her, Professor P?" Tara asked.

"Thanks," Professor P replied as he reached out to take Dotty.

"I thought all dinosaurs were big and scary," Brains said, looking at Dotty, puzzled.

"Not all of them, Brains," Professor P laughed. "Dotty's a very friendly dinosaur!"

"Eeek! Eeek!" Dotty cried and nibbled Professor P's hand.

"But she's definitely hungry," Professor P said, gently putting her down on the ground.

The little dinosaur was almost hidden in the tall plants that surrounded us. She waddled along, happily sniffing at the plants. As I watched her, I was surprised to see no grass anywhere. Instead, the ground was covered in green plants that had fine hair like leaves.

"I'm sure I've seen this before," I said bending down to examine one of the plants. "Do you know what it is, Professor P?"

"Yes, it's called marestail," Professor P replied, "It's a very common plant in the countryside at home. Amazing to think it's lasted for so many millions of years!"

Dotty continued wandering through the field of marestail and came to a yellow brown rubbery shrub. She sniffed at it curiously and then moved on to another bush with spiky leaves. As I watched her, I noticed there were no flowers either, only yellow, green and brown plants.

Tara interrupted my thoughts. "Dotty isn't eating anything," she said concerned. "I think they're still the wrong kind of plants."

I tried to remember the name of the plant we had found on the internet. What was it?

"Cycadeoid," I said. "That's what she eats. They must be here somewhere."

"What do they look like?" Professor P asked.

"A bit like ferns," Tara replied.

"I expect they grow in a forest, then," Professor P said thoughtfully.

I glanced around. We were looking down on a plain thinly covered with small trees and bushes. At the far side of the plain, were two flat hills. Through the gap between the hills, I could see a large forest in the far distance. I could just make out dinosaurs grazing at the edge of the forest.

"Over there," I said excitedly.

Floppy flew into the air and put a huge pair of purple binoculars to his eyes.

"Well spotted, Peter!" he cried. "It's a herd of diplodocus. There must be at least twenty."

"That's the place then!" Professor P said confidently. "Let's go!"

"What about those nasty dinosaurs, Professor P?" Brains asked nervously. "Those big scary ones?"

"I think we probably frightened them away," Professor P replied. "But, Peter, Tara, get the dino defences ready in case we need them again."

"OK!" we chorused.

Tara picked up Dotty and we all crammed back into the car. Brains and Sleepy sat in the front and Tara, Dotty, Sparky and I squeezed into the back. Floppy perched on Professor P's shoulder and scanned the horizon through his big purple binoculars.

"Hold tight!" Professor P called out, as he started the engine.

I felt a surge of excitement as the car shot forwards. We were off on our Jurassic journey at last! Off to explore the world of the dinosaurs and see things that no one had ever seen before. What an incredible adventure this was turning out to be!

Sparky was excited too. He jumped up, put his paws on the front seat and wagged his tail. His ears flapped in the wind as we sped along. I glanced excitedly at Tara. She smiled back, her eyes shining in anticipation.

"Peter, maybe we'll see a real scelidosaurus," she said excitedly.

"That would be amazing!" I replied. It seemed ages since we had found our fossil dinosaur on the beach. And now we might find a real live one!

"What does a scelidosaurus look like?" Professor P asked, interestedly.

"Well, I'm not exactly sure," Tara replied. "We've only ever seen part of a fossil but…"

"Scelidosaurus is an ornithischian dinosaur," Floppy interrupted, "of the suborder thyreophora…"

"Sounds like you swallowed a dictionary, Floppy!" Tara chuckled.

"A database to be precise," Floppy replied smugly. "I downloaded a Jurassic database from the internet before we left."

"Very clever of you, Floppy," Professor P said, pleased. "Do tell us more about the scelidosaurs," he added.

"It is a herbivorous quadruped…" Floppy began.

"A herbishous what?" Brains asked blankly.

"Herbivorous means it eats plants," Floppy replied. "And quadruped means it walks on four legs. Let me show you…"

Floppy appeared as a teacher wearing a black gown and a funny square hat with a tassel on it. A large dinosaur popped into the air beside him.

"Notice the small head, short neck and leaf-shaped teeth," Floppy said, pointing to them with a long ruler. "It also has a long stiff tail and is well armoured."

"Excellent, Floppy!" Professor P chuckled. "You can be our tour guide and tell us about all the dinosaurs we see."

"Thank you, Professor P," Floppy replied proudly. He immediately changed into an owl wearing a khaki safari suit and a large round white hat.

Floppy cleared his throat and then began his lecture. "The dinosaurs that attacked us are called allosaurs," he said authoritatively. "Allosaurs are bipedal carnivores belonging to the suborder theropoda and order saurschia…"

"What was that bit in the middle, Floppy?" Brains asked puzzled.

"Sorry, Brains," Floppy apologised. "I got a bit carried away. I'll try keep it simple!"

Tara looked at me and giggled. Floppy could be more funny when he was trying to be serious than when he was trying to be funny!

As we drove along, I heard a loud cry overhead. It sounded like a seagull. I looked up and saw a huge creature flying high above us. It glided effortlessly in the slight breeze, hardly moving its huge wings.

"Look up there!" I said excitedly.

I noticed more of them in the far distance, circling over the plains.

"It's a pterosaur," Floppy explained as the creature approached, "a flying reptile with a wing span of over ten metres…"

"Ten metres!" Professor P exclaimed, quickly glancing up at it. "That's over twice the length of this car!"

"A pterosaur is a meat eater…" Floppy continued.

"Is it dangerous?" Tara asked anxiously, clutching Dotty tightly to her chest.

"No," Floppy replied. "It eats only fish and scavenges for dead animals."

Tara looked relieved.

"I wish I'd brought my sketch book," she said, staring up at the creature. "I'd love to draw it. It would be great for our dinosaur exhibition guide."

As she spoke, Professor P reached into the side compartment of his door and took out a pen and a few sheets of paper.

"Here, Tara," he said, passing them to her. "The sheets are a bit crumpled, I'm afraid…"

"That's OK," she said, delighted, "thanks."

Tara passed Dotty to me. The little dinosaur sat on my lap and looked out of the car curiously.

Tara smoothed out the sheets of paper and began sketching the pterosaur. I watched as her hand flew over the paper and she perfectly captured the creature as it circled above us.

We drove through the pass between the hills and out into the large open plain. I gasped in astonishment at the incredible sight! Hundreds of dinosaurs of all shapes and sizes were grazing on the plain.

"Amazing!" Professor P said as he slowed the car so we could take a better look. "Have you ever seen anything like it?"

"This is absolutely…" Floppy cried. "Where to begin…I'm lost for words!"

"That's a first," I whispered to Tara.

Floppy did not take long to recover! He cleared his throat and continued with his commentary.

"If you would kindly turn to your right," he said in a professional tour guide voice, "you will see a herd of stegosaurs."

I turned my head and saw a group of about a dozen huge dinosaurs. They had bright orange plates on their backs and long spiky tails. They were walking very slowly with their heads close to the ground, munching contentedly at the plants.

Tara quickly pulled out a new sheet of paper and started sketching the animals.

"Amazing colour," she said in wonder. "I wish I'd brought my crayons."

"The orange plates on their backs act as a warning to other dinosaurs," Floppy explained.

"I wouldn't like to have an argument with one!" Brains said anxiously. "Those tails look pretty dangerous."

"Correct," Floppy replied. "A direct hit from one of their tails can kill a fully grown allosaurus."

"Don't get too close, Professor P!" Brains warned nervously.

"Don't worry, Brains, I won't," Professor P replied, steering the car away from them.

As we drove slowly across the plain, Floppy told us the names of all the dinosaurs and a few facts about each one. I tried to take in everything I could. The long necked dinosaurs reaching up to the tops of the trees were called brachiosaurs. The smaller dinosaurs, about my height and with sharp beaks were called dryosaurs. Floppy told us so many interesting things, I hoped I would remember them all for our dinosaur guide!

We had crossed most of the plain now and had almost reached the herd of diplodocus. They stood by the edge of the forest, their long tails waving gracefully as they grazed on the trees.

"The diplodocus is one of the longest animals ever to have lived," Floppy said as we approached the herd. "Their tails can grow up to fourteen metres in length."

"Good heavens!" Professor P exclaimed. "That's longer than my house!"

"When attacked, they use their tails like whips," Floppy continued. "The tips can reach speeds up to a thousand miles an hour."

Tara stopped sketching and stared at the huge creatures.

"So Dotty's going to grow into one of those!" she cried, in amazement. "I just can't imagine how…"

"She's going to have to eat an awful lot!" I exclaimed.

"Correct," Floppy said. "Young diplodocus gain about two kilograms every day. When they leave the safety of the forest at the end of their first year they will weigh as much as a rhino."

As we approached the herd, Tara picked up her pen and continued sketching. One of the diplodocus turned and took a step towards us. I could feel the ground shake under its enormous weight.

"It's going to squash us," Brains wailed. "I don't want to get flattened, Professor P."

"It's just curious, Brains," Professor P said kindly as he stopped the car. "It won't harm us."

141

I watched in awe as the huge creature slowly approached. It curved its neck down towards us and made a deep bellowing sound.

Dotty jumped off my lap and scrambled up onto the front seat to see what was happening.

"Eeek! Eeek!" she cried when she saw the diplodocus peering down at us.

"No, Dotty!" Tara said, grabbing hold of her to stop her getting out of the car.

The diplodocus stared at Dotty curiously and then it slowly turned away. It plodded back to the trees and continued grazing.

Professor P started the car again and we skirted around the herd of dinosaurs towards the forest. As we got closer, I could see tall pine trees and higher up the slope, enormous trees with reddish bark that towered into the sky.

Professor P stopped the car at the edge of the forest. Dotty cried out eagerly when she saw the trees. She seemed to know this was her home. At last, she would have something to eat!

CHAPTER EIGHTEEN

Forest Foray

"We made it!" Professor P said happily as he got out of the car.

Tara picked up Dotty and we jumped out of the car. Sleepy and Sparky ran over towards the trees and wagged their tails expectantly. Only Brains remained in the front seat, fumbling with the catch on his seatbelt. Floppy flapped around impatiently trying to help him.

"Eeek! Eeek!" Dotty cried, sniffing the air excitedly.

"You'll soon have something to eat, Dotty!" Tara said, reassuringly.

"Come on, Sparky," I said. "Let's go!"

"Wait!" Floppy cried, blocking our way and holding up a large stop sign. "Dinosaurs are probably lurking in the forest, hiding in the trees, just waiting to pounce!"

I glanced nervously at the woods. Tara clutched Dotty tightly to her chest. Suddenly the forest did not seem so welcoming!

"One of the most dangerous predators is ornitholestes," Floppy continued. "It's two metres in length with long grasping hands, vicious claws and…"

"Can I go home now, please, Professor P?" Brains interrupted.

"You'll be all right, Brains," Floppy said, dismissively. "You're made of metal! Dotty's the one who is in danger. She's too small to protect herself."

"You're right, Floppy," Professor P said thoughtfully. "We'd better take our dino defences."

Professor P leant over the car and picked up the metal box from the back seat.

"I don't think the power balls will be much use in a forest," he said as he rummaged through the box. "They need hard ground to bounce properly and they'd probably get caught up in the branches. But the sonic torches will come in useful."

Professor P gave the torches to Tara and me. Then he took out a small cone made of clear plastic with a shiny silver base.

"What's that?" I asked.

"It's a Scare Strobe," he explained. "It sends out a bright pulsing light which should frighten any dinosaurs away. It'll work well in the darkness of the forest."

Professor P put the cone in his pocket and closed the box.

"Well, I think we should be safe from attack now," he said confidently.

As we started towards the forest, Brains hung back, reluctant to follow.

"Eh, excuse me, Professor P," he said timidly. "But about those dinosaurs. The scary ones lurking in the forest…"

"Would you rather stay here and guard the car, Brains?" Professor P asked tactfully.

"Yes, Professor P," Brains replied, sounding much happier. "I've had enough dinosaurs for today."

"Make sure you stay here though, Brains," Professor P warned. "Don't go wandering off and getting lost! Unless, of course, there's an emergency."

"OK," Brains replied. "I've got it. Stay here. Don't get lost. Unless there's an emergency."

"Come on! Let's get going," Floppy cried impatiently. He changed into full safari gear, with ridiculously large walking boots.

Sparky barked and look up at me questioningly. He did not understand why we were taking so long. He just wanted to go exploring!

"All right, Sparky," I said as we finally set off. "We're going now."

He wagged his tail eagerly and bounded off along a rough track into the forest.

"Sparky!" I called after him. "Wait for us!"

"Woof!" he barked indignantly as I put him on the lead.

Professor P, Sleepy and Floppy led the way into the forest with me, Tara, Dotty and Sparky close behind. Sparky tugged at his lead, excited by all the forest smells.

He buried his nose in a group of tall ferns and sniffed at all the trees.

When we were safely in the forest, Tara put Dotty on the ground. The little dinosaur wagged her tail happily and darted ahead through the ferns. Her brown and green colouring was an excellent camouflage – she blended in perfectly with the undergrowth.

We continued deeper into the woods and I felt very relieved to be out of the scorching heat of the plain. The forest was a beautiful place; dappled sunlight trickled down through the tops of the trees. It was an amazing sight, just like being in a natural cathedral.

As we walked through the woods, I looked around curiously. A small lizard ran along a tree branch, jumped off and darted into the ferns. A beautiful moth like insect with long silver wings fluttered past. It was all very different from the woods at home.

Suddenly Floppy flew over to us.

"Don't move!" he whispered. "There's an apatosaurus ahead."

"Is it dangerous?" Tara asked as she quickly picked up Dotty

"No, it's a herbivore," Floppy replied, "But we don't want to frighten it."

I grabbed hold of Sparky's collar and held my breath excitedly. Then, through the trees, I saw it! The dinosaur was about the size of a large horse, with a very long neck and tiny head. It moved slowly across our path, nibbling the ferns, unaware of our presence.

"It's only a baby apatosaurs," Floppy whispered, "but it will soon grow enormous. They're the largest land animals ever to have lived, weighing in at over thirty five tonnes!"

"That's more than four elephants!" Professor P exclaimed.

"In a few months time it will be too big for the forest," Floppy continued. "Then, when it wants to eat ferns, it will have to knock down the trees to get to them."

After a few minutes, the apatosaurus passed and we continued on our way. We soon came to a clearing in the woods. Rising above the ferns were some bushes that I had not seen before.

"Ah, ha!" Floppy cried, peering at one of the bushes through a large magnifying glass.

"What is it, Floppy?" I asked.

"Notice the bisporangiate strobili," Floppy replied.

We all looked at him blankly.

"The cones!" he replied. "Look at the shape. They're definitely cycadeoids!"

The plants had thick woody stems and palm-like leaves with small furry orange cones. Dotty ran over to one of the plants and began devouring the leaves hungrily.

"At last!" Tara cried.

We watched as Dotty chomped away at the bush and then moved onto another.

"She certainly eats a lot," I said as Dotty stripped the second plant.

We were all happily watching Dotty, when suddenly Sleepy began to growl in warning. Sparky jumped up too, the hairs on his back bristling. He cocked his head and listened intently.

"What's the matter, Sparky?" I asked, standing up and looking around.

There was nothing to be seen. But then I heard a crack, a twig snapped. Something had moved in the undergrowth. I spun around as I heard another rustling sound behind me.

"We're surrounded!" Tara cried out in panic.

"Form a circle," Professor P ordered firmly.

Tara quickly grabbed Dotty and we all stood in a circle, our backs together, so we could see in all directions. I held tightly onto Sparky's collar.

"Get the sonic torches ready," Professor P said quietly, "but don't switch them on yet. Wait till I give the order."

I took the sonic torch out of my pocket and pointed it towards the rustling sound. I gripped it tightly with my finger poised over the red button.

"Any idea what to expect, Floppy?" Professor P asked as he took the Scare Strobe cone out of his pocket

"It's probably a group of the ornitholestes, I told you about earlier," Floppy replied. "They're vicious meat-eaters, perfectly designed for hunting in the undergrowth. They can dart in and out of the trees, snatching their prey in an instant."

I heard another rustling sound close by. Something was waiting to pounce!

"Over there!" I cried, pointing to the nearest tree to my right.

148

My hands were shaking as I raised the sonic torch and took aim. Then, out from behind the tree, it came.

"A baby diplodocus!" I exclaimed.

Tara let out a sigh of relief.

"Oh, Floppy!" Professor P laughed. "You had us all worked up!"

"Sorry, Professor P, easy enough mistake to make," Floppy said with a shrug.

"True," Professor P chuckled.

The baby diplodocus waddled into the centre of the clearing. It nibbled peacefully at the bushes, completely unaware of us.

"Look, there's another one," Tara whispered as a second, slightly larger diplodocus came out of the trees.

Soon, a whole group of baby diplodocus had gathered! Tara put Dotty down on the ground. She went over to join them and they sniffed each other in greeting.

"I think she's made some new friends!" I said as the dinosaurs munched away at the plants together.

"I've never seen her look so happy," Tara said thoughtfully.

Professor P glanced at his watch.

"I think we need to get moving," he said, "if we're going to collect some plants for Dotty and get you home in time for tea…"

"Are you sure we can't stay longer, Professor P?" Tara asked. "Dotty's so happy. I don't like to take her away from her new friends."

"Well, perhaps, just a few minutes," Professor P agreed with a smile, "but I don't want to make you late…"

"But we *can* stay as long as we like, Professor P," Floppy interrupted, "and still be home for tea."

Tara and I looked blankly at Floppy.

"We're time travellers aren't we?" Floppy said. "It shouldn't be a problem to lose a few hours on our way home, should it?"

"Oh, I see what you mean, Floppy!" Professor P replied. "Yes, that's a very interesting idea!"

I looked at Tara, puzzled.

"What…?" I began.

"Floppy is suggesting that we change the way the portal works," Professor P explained.

"Exactly," Floppy said excitedly.

"As it stands, the portal works as a time bridge," Professor P explained, "so for every hour we spend here, an hour will have passed at home."

"But it doesn't have to be like that!" Floppy added.

"No, it doesn't," Professor P nodded in agreement. "We can reprogram the portal to returns us to whenever we want."

"Oh, wouldn't it be fun to get back *before* we left," Floppy exclaimed. "We'd meet ourselves…"

"Now, let's not get carried away, Floppy," Professor P exclaimed. "Who knows what would happen if we tried that! But we can certainly change the portal so it returns us shortly after we left. Then only a few minutes will have passed at home."

"Exactly," Floppy said confidently. "We could even…" he paused. "Professor P!" he continued excitedly, "have you still got your adventure inventions in the car?"

"Yes, Floppy," Professor P replied questioningly.

"Then we could stay here overnight!" Floppy cried, flapping around excitedly. "We could have a Jurassic camp!"

"Oh, yes," Tara and I cried, delighted. "Please can we stay, Professor P?"

Professor P laughed.

"All right," he said with a smile, "tonight, we'll camp in the forest!"

CHAPTER NINETEEN

Camping

We were going to spend the night in the forest!

"Brilliant!" Tara and I cried excitedly.

Floppy turned cartwheels in the air. "Oh, goody," he cried. "I love camping – I'll get out my hammock!"

"Well, that's settled," Professor P said happily. "No time to lose! We'll need to set up our camp before it gets dark."

We hurriedly filled our rucksacks with leaves for Dotty. When we had finished, Tara bent down and picked up Dotty.

"Eek! Eek!" the little dinosaur cried indignantly.

"It's all right, Dotty," Tara said reassuringly. "We'll come back and see your friends again."

Dotty looked up at Tara trusting. She seemed to understand.

We left the clearing and walked quickly through the forest, eager to begin our camping adventure. When we arrived at the car, Brains rushed over to greet us.

"Oh, you're safe!" he cried. "You were so long, I thought you'd been eaten by dinosaurs!"

"No need to worry, Brains!" Professor P chuckled.

"So can we go home now?" Brains pleaded.

"No, we're going to camp here!" Floppy said excitedly.

Brains did not seem at all pleased with this news!

"Are you sure it's safe?" he asked, glancing around nervously. "What about the scary dinosaurs?"

"Don't worry, Brains," Floppy said. "Most dinosaurs are cold blooded, so they sleep at night."

Brains paused for a moment to think about this.

"Good!" he said finally.

Professor P opened the boot of the car and took out a red rucksack. The words, *Adventure Inventions* were written in gold letters on the front.

"What's in the bag, Professor P?" I asked intrigued.

"In this small rucksack, you'll find everything you need for an adventure," Professor P replied, with a twinkle in his eye.

"And more besides!" Floppy added excitedly.

"All set then!" Professor P said as he put the rucksack on his back.

"Just a minute," Tara said as she reached into the back seat.

She took out the cardboard box and carefully put Dotty inside.

"I don't want Dotty to get lost!" she said, closing the lid.

Professor P strode into the woods with Floppy flying ahead, holding a lantern to light the way. Sleepy and Sparky followed, wagging their tails happily, knowing more adventure was afoot! Tara and I rushed after them and Brains followed at the rear.

After a short walk, we came to a clearing in the woods. It was about twenty metres wide and covered in ferns.

"This will do just fine," Professor P said, looking around carefully.

Professor P took off the rucksack and unzipped one of the side compartments. I looked on in anticipation as he took out a large purple penknife. Written on the side were the words *Professor P's Patented Penknife (Purple)*.

"Electric penknife," he explained, pulling out a small blade with a serrated edge. "Ideal for cutting up firewood. Can you to start gathering logs now, please, Brains?

"Yes, Professor P," Brains replied and marched off into the woods with Floppy lighting the way.

Professor P called after them, "Oh, and get some long thin branches so I can make a shelter."

"Now, let's see, what else do I have...?" Professor P continued, reaching into the main compartment of the rucksack.

He pulled out a black box with the words *Total Tent* written on it.

"Self-inflating tent," Professor P explained proudly. "No messing about with pegs and poles. It goes up in an instant!"

"What a good idea!" Tara exclaimed happily.

"You and Peter can share it," Professor P added. "There's enough room for both of you."

"Great," we chorused, delighted.

We found a flat piece of ground near the edge of the clearing for the tent. Then we cleared the ferns and brushed away the pinecones.

"How does it work?" I asked as Professor P put the Total Tent box down in the cleared area.

"Press the red button," Professor P replied, "stand well clear and you'll see!"

I pressed the button and we all quickly retreated. A few seconds later, a loud hissing sound came from the box and the black casing split open. A green tent burst out, like half a balloon. When it reached full size, there was a series of sharp bangs and tent pegs flew into the ground. It was all over in a matter of seconds!

"Brilliant!" Tara and I cried, rushing over to the tent.

We unzipped the front and looked inside. The tent had a main living area and two small bedrooms. We crawled inside excitedly.

"Look, Peter!" Tara cried as she unzipped the bedroom door. "It's even got sleeping bags!"

It was perfect!

Tara took Dotty out of her box and put her in the tent. The little creature looked around curiously.

"Do you like our tent, Dotty?" Tara asked kindly.

The little dinosaur just yawned, tired by the long day. Tara and I made her a bed of ferns at the end of one of the sleeping bags. She laid down and fell asleep almost instantly.

When we came out of the tent, Floppy and Brains had returned. Brains was laden with branches and thick logs. He dropped them with a clatter.

"Well done, Brains!" Professor P said encouragingly. "Keep up the good work!"

"Thank you, Professor P," Brains replied, pleased.

Brains and Floppy went into the forest to get more wood. Professor P showed us how his electric penknife worked and we started sawing up the logs. When we had enough wood, Tara and I built the fire in the centre of the clearing. We worked hard in the fading light with some enthusiastic help from Sleepy and Sparky!

While we were building the fire, Professor P worked on his A-frame shelter. He pushed branches into the ground and expertly wove them together at the top. When the shelter was almost finished, Sleepy ran inside. She lay down, panting, tired from her exertions in the heat.

Floppy strung a rainbow coloured hammock between our tent and Professor P's shelter. He swung back and forth in it, lazily sipping a bright orange drink through a long straw.

"Ah, this is the life!" he sighed as he watched us all hard at work. Tara and I laughed!

It was dark when we finished the camp. Tired, but happy Tara, Sparky and I sat down by the fireplace. Professor P lit the fire and the dry kindling immediately burst into flames.

"Now let's see what we have in here," he said, opening his rucksack. "Excellent. We've enough food for tonight and breakfast tomorrow."

Professor P handed out plastic bowls and cutlery, "Hungry, anyone?" he asked.

We nodded eagerly. I was famished!

"Would you like to try some Super Soup?" Professor P asked as he took some cans out of his rucksack.

"Yes, please," we said hungrily.

"I've got tangy tomato or…" he peered at the label, "parsnip and pineapple."

"Pineapple!" Tara exclaimed.

"It is rather an unusual flavour," Professor P admitted with a slight grimace.

"I think I'll have the tomato, please, Professor P," Tara said politely.

"Me too," I added quickly.

"Wise decision," Floppy called over from his hammock.

"I'd like the pineapple one, Professor P!" Brains said, not wanting to be left out.

"Don't be silly, Brains!" Floppy chided him, "You're a robot. You don't eat!"

"Oh, yes, I forgot," Brains said, scratching his head.

Professor P put the cans down on the ground a short distance away from us.

"Self-heating can," he explained. "Press the red button and wait ten seconds for it to warm up."

"If it doesn't explode first," Floppy quipped.

"Now, now, Floppy," Professor P admonished as he pressed the buttons on the cans and quickly stepped back.

Brains also stepped backwards and nervously put his fingers in his ears. Sparky nuzzled up to me and I put my arm safely around him.

But there was no need to worry! The self-heating cans worked perfectly! Professor P peeled off the tops of the cans to reveal steaming soup. And the smell was wonderful!

Brains took his fingers out of his ears. "It worked!" he said in surprise.

"That's a first!" Floppy added.

"Of course it worked," Professor P said, sounding slightly offended.

Professor P poured the soup into our bowls and passed round some slices of bread. Tara and I tucked in eagerly. Professor P filled a bowl of water for the dogs and gave them a small bag of dog biscuits each. Sparky lay down contentedly at my feet when he had finished.

"That was brilliant!" Tara said as she mopped her bowl with the last piece of bread.

157

"Thanks," Professor P smiled appreciatively. "I always think food tastes so much better when you're outside, especially round a campfire."

"Me to," I agreed.

"Anyone for pudding?" Professor P asked. "Turnip trifle or strawberry jelly?"

"Er, jelly, please," Tara and I replied, trying not to laugh.

Floppy returned to his hammock. As we continued eating, he swung back and forth, sipping his cocktail and trying to look cool again.

After the meal, we sat around the fire chatting excitedly about all the dinosaurs we had seen. I could have stayed there all night, gazing into the flames and enjoying the peace of the forest.

Eventually though, it was time for bed. We washed up and put everything away safely in the rucksack.

"Brains, you stay here on guard with Floppy," Professor P said as he walked to his shelter. "Keep the fire going, but don't get too close. I don't want you overheating!"

"I won't, Professor P," Brains replied, prodding the fire with a long stick.

"I'm certainly going to sleep well tonight," I said as we walked away from the fire.

"Me too," Tara agreed, yawning.

"Night, night," Floppy called out. "Don't let the bed dinosaurs bite!"

Professor P squeezed into his shelter. Sleepy lay down outside, guarding the entrance.

Tara, Sparky and I climbed into our tent. Sparky lay down peacefully on the ferns next to Dotty.

"Night, Tara," I said as I climbed into my sleeping bag.

"Night, Peter," she yawned in reply.

I curled up in my sleeping bag and listened to the comforting crackling sound from the fire. As I dozed off, all the amazing events of the day floated through my mind.

What a fantastic adventure it had been!

CHAPTER TWENTY

Difficult Decision

The next morning, I woke with a start as Sparky jumped onto my sleeping bag.

"Hi, Sparky," I said, giving him a pat on the head.

He wagged his tail excitedly, ready and eager to start the day.

I crawled into the main compartment of the tent and called to Tara. There was no reply, so I popped my head into her sleeping compartment. She sat up and rubbed her eyes.

"Hi, Peter," she said, yawning.

"Sleep well?" I asked, noticing dark bags under her eyes.

"I couldn't get to sleep," she replied, "I was worried about Dotty…"

"Dotty?" I said puzzled, "but she's fine now."

I glanced at the little dinosaur lying asleep, curled up on a pile of leaves beside Tara's sleeping bag.

"I guess so," Tara said, looking down at her.

Tara did not seem her usual self this morning. She was normally so bright and bubbly. I wondered what was wrong.

Sparky nudged me playfully, then ran to the tent door and barked impatiently.

"OK, Sparky," I said, "I'm coming!"

I unzipped the tent door and Sparky rushed out. I climbed out after him and looked around. It was already very warm with just a slight breeze swaying the tops of the trees.

A few moments later, Tara climbed out of the tent. She stood up and stretched her arms.

"Another lovely day," she said with a yawn.

We stood for a while, enjoying the sights and smells of this beautiful forest. It felt incredible to be here, surrounded by the enormous redwood trees. I could hardly believe we were really in a Jurassic forest!

As we stood admiring the view, I noticed a faint snoring sound. Snoring? I turned round and noticed Floppy lying in his hammock. His long rabbit ears were draped over his eyes and were rising and falling in time with the snoring. I had to laugh – he was pretending to be asleep!

Tara and I went over to the fire and sat down beside Professor P.

"Morning, Peter, morning, Tara," he greeted us with a smile. "Sleep well?"

"Yes, the tent's great!" I replied enthusiastically.

Tara did not reply.

"All right, Tara," Professor P asked, looking at her, concerned.

"Sure," she replied, "I'll be fine when I've had some breakfast."

"Well, help yourselves," Professor P said, passing us a plate each. "Toast and peanut butter all right?"

"Thanks," we said, reaching out for the slices of bread.

It was great fun toasting the slices of bread in the fire. I had to scrape the burnt bits off my piece but with a thick spread of peanut butter, it tasted great!

Brains came over and sat down by the fire. He looked at the toast curiously.

"I wish... I wish I could eat toast," he said, quietly. "I think... I feel hungry."

He spoke slowly and with difficulty, slurring his words together. I looked at him, concerned and wondered what was wrong.

"Oh, dear, I think you're getting low on power, Brains," Professor P said. "I haven't had a chance to recharge your battery, yet. I'll have to put you on charge when we get back to the car."

"Thank you, Professor P," Brains said slowly after a short pause.

Tara and I helped ourselves to more toast, while Professor P drank his tea. I felt so happy, sitting round the campfire, surrounded by such an amazing forest.

After breakfast, we began clearing everything away. Tara and I washed up the breakfast things and packed them into the rucksack while Professor P put out the fire. He poured water on the glowing embers and then covered them with earth.

While Professor P was making the fire safe, Tara and I went over to the tent. Tara unzipped the flap and Dotty jumped out, looking happy and refreshed from her sleep.

We pulled the tent pegs out of the ground and then tried to work out how to take the tent apart. Floppy flew over, eager to help.

"Look for a red *Pull Me* tab," he said. "It's underneath the tent."

"Thanks, Floppy," I said, lifting the tent.

Tara pulled the tab. We jumped back as a loud hissing sound filled the air and watched in amazement as the tent gradually folded in on itself. Professor P had thought of everything!

After a few minutes, the tent had completely deflated. We stuffed it back in its box and took it over to Professor P.

"All done," I said, handing him the box.

"Thanks," he said as he packed the box into his rucksack. "I'll take everything back to the car and sort out Brains while you collect some plants for Dotty."

"OK," we agreed.

"We'll need to bring back plenty!" I added.

"Yes, she'll grow up very fast," Professor P agreed. "In a few months she'll be too big for your house, Tara!"

Tara nodded. "I know," she said quietly.

I looked at Tara. She still did not seem her usual happy self this morning and I wondered what was wrong. Was she just tired?

"Floppy, you go with Peter and Tara while they collect the leaves," Professor P said as he put on his rucksack.

"Aye, aye, captain," Floppy replied. "I'll keep a look out for danger!"

Floppy changed into a fluffy pink parrot and held a large telescope to his right eye. I laughed at his silly expression.

"See if you can bring back some whole plants too," Professor P said. "I know some plant experts at Cambridge who'll be able to help me grow more of them. They'll be in for a surprise!" he added with a twinkle in his eye.

Professor P reached into his rucksack and took out two small trowels.

"Here you are," he said, giving them to us, "you can use these to dig up the plants. They're telescopic spades. Just press the button on the handle to make them as long as you like!"

I chuckled. Professor P never had anything ordinary! Finally, he gave us a handful of carrier bags and we were ready to go.

"Remember to keep Sleepy and Sparky with you at all times so you don't get lost," he added, "and don't forget the sonic torches, just in case."

"Don't worry, I'll take care of them, Professor P," Floppy said seriously.

"Well, we're all set then," Professor P said with a smile. "See you at the car in about an hour?"

"OK," we replied.

"Come along, Brains!" Professor P called as he strode off towards the car. "Let's get you on charge."

"Slow...down...Professor P!" Brains said pathetically. "I...can't...keep...up...with...you!"

Tara and I went in the opposite direction, deeper into the forest. Dotty led the way, wagging her tail happily, as she walked through the ferns. Sparky and Sleepy kept close to our sides and Floppy flew ahead of us, scanning the forest with his telescope.

We soon came to a small clearing with plenty of cycadeoid plants. Dotty rushed over to one of the plants and began to eat it eagerly. Tara stood watching Dotty.

I bent down and started to fill the bags with leaves.

"Anything the matter, Tara?" I asked tentatively, after a few minutes.

Tara shook her head and then bent down to help. We soon filled two bags and began to dig up a small bush. It was tiring work, trying to break up the hard earth with the small spades. Sleepy and Sparky scrabbled at the ground, trying to help. Floppy flew around, offering us his usual helpful advice!

We had not made much progress, when Floppy suddenly squawked, "Dotty's gone!"

I glanced around. There was no sign of the little dinosaur anywhere.

"Dotty, where are you?" Tara called out anxiously.

"Sleepy, Sparky, find Dotty," I said pointing to where we had last seen her.

Sparky barked and dashed off with Sleepy and Floppy close behind. Tara and I ran after them, trying to keep up as they raced through the thick undergrowth. Moments later, the dogs stopped and waited for us at the edge of another clearing, their tails wagging. They had found Dotty!

She was munching contentedly on the plants. But she was not alone. By her side was another diplodocus, about twice as big.

"She's found a new friend!" Floppy said, peering at them through his telescope.

Floppy was right. It looked as though the larger dinosaur was watching over Dotty, protecting her.

I started to walk towards Dotty.

"No, Peter," Tara said, taking my arm. "Leave her."

I stared at Tara in surprise. She looked down, unable to meet my gaze.

"I don't think we should take Dotty home," she began, her voice shaking.

I stared at Tara in astonishment.

"That's why I couldn't sleep last night," she explained. "I was thinking about Dotty. She won't be happy if we take her back with us."

"But, Tara…" I began.

"I started to think about it yesterday," Tara continued, "when we saw the big group of diplodocus. Dotty's a herd animal, she'll be lonely without any others of her kind…"

Tara broke off, tears welling up in her eyes.

"I'd love to keep her, Peter," she continued, "more than anything, but I know it's best for her to stay here. Look how happy she is, I've made up my mind. I'll say one last goodbye and then we'll leave her here."

I nodded, unable to speak. I felt so upset for Tara. I could not imagine what it would be like for me to give up Sparky. But I also knew Tara was right. This was Dotty's home; this was where she belonged, in her own time, with others of her kind.

Tara slowly walked into the centre of the clearing. She knelt down beside Dotty. The little dinosaur turned and looked up at Tara with her big soft eyes.

"Goodbye, Dotty," Tara said quietly. "I'll never forget you."

"Eeek!" Dotty cried, nuzzling up to Tara.

Then Dotty went back to munching the leaves. Tara stood up and watched her for a few moments longer. Then she turned away.

"Let's go," she said quietly.

I called to Sparky and Sleepy and we set off, back to the clearing where we had collected the plants. When we arrived, Tara picked up the bags and emptied the leaves onto the ground.

"Won't be needing these," she said, putting the empty bags into her pocket.

We put the soil back around the plants and packed away the spades.

I called to Sparky but he hung back. He glanced over in the direction we had left Dotty and then looked at me questioningly.

DIFFICULT DECISION

"Dotty's not coming with us, Sparky," I said. "She's staying here with her new friends."

He seemed to understand. He ran over and we walked back through the woods in silence.

CHAPTER TWENTY ONE

Jurassic Jet

When we reached the edge of the forest, I stopped and turned to Tara.

"All right?" I asked, concerned.

"Sure," she replied quietly. "Let's go home now."

We stepped out of the cool forest into the hot sunlight. I looked around for Professor P, squinting in the bright light. Over to the right, I noticed a large group of trees had been knocked to the ground. It almost looked like a hurricane had struck the forest. And in the midst of the devastation was...

"The car!" I cried in horror.

"It's crushed!" Floppy screeched in dismay.

Floppy flew down the hill towards the car. Sparky barked and ran after him with me and Tara in close pursuit. When we reached the car, I could see how badly it had been damaged. A tall pine tree had fallen onto the boot and crushed it. One of the wheels was twisted at an awkward angle. Professor P was bending down by the car, examining the damage. Floppy flew over to the Professor P and perched on his shoulder.

"Professor P! What happened?" Tara and I cried.

"Apatosaurs," he replied. "A herd of apatosaurs. They've moved on now but the damage is done…"

He looked up at us and stopped abruptly.

"You didn't get any plants?" he said, puzzled, noticing our hands were empty.

"I decided to leave Dotty here." Tara replied sadly.

Professor P looked at her and nodded in understanding. "I think you've made the right decision, Tara," he said kindly. "She'll be happier here."

Tara smiled bravely.

"What are we going to do about the car, Professor P?" Tara asked, quickly changing the subject.

"Can you fix it?" I added anxiously.

"It looks bad," Floppy said gloomily. "Very bad."

"I'm afraid it does," Professor P agreed. "First, we have to get the tree off the car so I can find out how bad the damage is. We'll need Brains' help – hopefully he'll have enough charge by now."

I noticed Brains lying on his back in the sun. A dark blue solar panel lay on the ground beside him. Professor P went over to Brains and switched him on. His arms and legs jerked into life and he sat bolt upright

"How are you feeling, Brains?" Professor P asked.

Brains moved his head from side to side and then stood up.

"As good as new, Professor P!" he replied, his eyes shining brightly.

"Excellent!" Professor P said happily. "We're going to need your help to move this tree."

"No, problem!" Brains said confidently, striding over to the tree.

"First, let's get the dogs out of harm's way," Professor P said. "I don't want to risk them getting hurt."

Professor P settled Sparky and Sleepy down in the shade of a tree with a bowl of water and some dog biscuits. I tied Sparky's lead to the tree for extra safety.

We all moved into position behind the tree. I put my hands under the trunk and braced myself.

"Take the strain!" Floppy shouted through a large megaphone. "On the count of three. One, two, three, lift!"

I pushed with all my strength and the tree began to move. The car let out a loud creaking noise as the tree rose up.

"I've got it!" Brains cried as he lifted the tree above his head.

He staggered forwards a few steps and then dropped the tree clear of the car.

We watched tensely as Professor P and Floppy examined the car. Professor P lay down on his back and slid underneath the car to look at the underside. He emerged a few moments later, looking unhappy.

"Is it bad, Professor P?" Tara asked.

"I'm afraid so," he replied with a sigh. "The rear axle has snapped, so I won't be able to drive it. I fear we'll have to leave the car here and walk back to the portal."

"Walk back," Brains repeated in alarm. "But what about those big scary dinosaurs?"

I glanced at Tara nervously. I did not like the idea of facing those allosaurus without the protection of the car!

"And we'll need the car when we've been through the portal, Professor P" Floppy reminded him. "Without the hovercraft, we'll be stranded on the island."

"Yes, that is a problem," Professor P nodded thoughtfully

"But will the car still work as a hovercraft, Professor P?" I asked unsure.

"Yes," he replied. "The hover fan hasn't been damaged. It's in the centre of the car and well protected."

"Can't we use the car as a hovercraft now?" Tara suggested.

"Unfortunately not," Professor P replied. "Hovercraft only work well on smooth surfaces, like water. It wouldn't have enough power to lift us over rough ground. But..."

Professor P broke off. A smile returned to his face and that familiar twinkle appeared in his eye. He was silent for a few moments, deep in thought. We waited expectantly – what was he thinking?

"I've got it!" he said finally. "With a bit of work, it can be done!"

"What?" I asked, curiously.

"You'll see," he replied mysteriously.

Professor P prised open the boot of the car and took out a large toolbox.

"I'll need your help, Brains," Professor P said. "First, I want you to make two large metal cones using the sheet metal from the lid of the boot."

"OK, Professor P," Brains nodded.

"Then I want you to weld the cones onto the back of the car," Professor P continued.

"Why?" Brains asked, puzzled.

"I know why!" Floppy burst out. "I know just what you're going to do, Professor P. What a brilliant idea!"

"Thank you," Professor P said modestly, "can I leave you in charge then, Floppy, while I'll start work on the fuel system?"

"I'm on it!" Floppy cried, changing into a car mechanic in oil stained overalls and holding a dirty white towel in his hands.

Professor P grabbed a handful of tools and disappeared under the car.

"Can we help, Floppy?" I asked eagerly.

"Yes," Floppy replied, "you can take off the back wheels."

I picked up a large cross spanner and we started undoing the wheel nuts. It was hard work in the heat of sun!

When we had removed the rear wheels of the car, we went over to see what Brains was doing. He had almost finished welding the two large cones onto the back of the car. What *was* it going to be, I wondered!

It took about an hour before the car was finished and Professor P completely satisfied it was safe.

"Let's get in and try it now," he said finally.

Tara and I went over to get Sparky and then climbed into the back seat of the car. Sparky jumped onto my lap and wagged his tail excitedly. Professor P got into the driver's seat and Sleepy jumped into the passenger seat beside him. Brains waited outside the car.

"Brains, I want you to light the fuel," Professor P ordered, giving him a lighter. "Be careful to stand to one side!"

"It'll make quite a bang!" Floppy warned, sprouting a large pair of earmuffs.

I looked at Tara in astonishment. Was Brains really going to set light to the petrol?

"Ready?" Professor P asked, turning to us. "Seatbelts on!"

Tara and I quickly put on our seatbelts. Professor P turned the key in the ignition and the engine roared into life.

"Switching to hovercraft mode!" he said as he pressed the red button on the dashboard.

I heard a thud as the rubber skirt dropped into place. Then the hover fan burst into action, sending air rushing out all around us. The car rose slightly, supported on a cushion of air.

"Here goes!" Professor P said as he pressed a yellow button on the dashboard.

The air filled with the unpleasant smell of petrol. It was terrible! I held my nose and tried not to breath.

"Light it now, Brains!" Professor P called out above the noise of the hover fan.

I turned round and saw Brains bend down behind the car.

BANG!

There was an enormous explosion! A huge ball of fire burst from the cones at the back of the car, knocking Brains to the ground. The car rocketed forward as two huge flames shot out from the rear.

Professor P immediately reached over to the dashboard and adjusted a dial. The flames died down and the car slowed to a halt.

"It worked!" Floppy squawked. "Well done, Professor P! It goes like a rocket!"

Brains ran over to the car. He was covered in soot and looked a mess!

"Wait for me, Professor P!" he cried pathetically.

"Are you all right, Brains?" Professor P asked, reaching across to open the passenger door.

"No," Brains replied as he collapsed into the front seat. "I forgot to stand to the side, like you said, Professor P."

Tara and I chuckled.

"I'll give you a proper check up when we get home," Professor P said kindly. "Right! Everybody ready?"

"Yes," we all chorused.

"I'll try it on full power," Professor P said, reaching out to the dashboard.

"Hold on to your hats!" Floppy cried as he put on a crash helmet and pair of goggles.

Professor P turned the dial fully to the right. I was caught off guard by the sudden deafening roar and heat from the flames. We were thrown back against the seats as the car accelerated.

Sparky yelped in surprise and I held onto him tightly. I could feel his heart pounding in fear.

The car sped faster and faster across the plain, shaking violently over the bumpy ground. When we reached top speed, we must have been going over a hundred miles an hour!

The dinosaurs that had been grazing so peacefully were terrified by the noise of the jet engine and a group of stegosaurs scattered in every direction.

"Watch out, Professor P!" I cried above the roar of the engine.

We were heading towards a herd of diplodocus grazing at the far end of the plain. The huge creatures looked up and bellowed loudly as we approached, frightened by the noise of the car.

Professor P slowed the car but could not to steer us away in time.

"I can't look!" Brains said, covering his eyes. "Tell me when it's over!"

I watched horrified as we hurtled straight towards the middle of the herd. The diplodocus were equally terrified, unable to get out of the way in time.

175

In a moment, we were among the herd, weaving our way though the huge creatures. It was mayhem! The dinosaurs fled in panic, running in all directions.

As we passed under the neck of one of the diplodocus, it let out a deafening cry.

"Duck!" Floppy cried, as a tail swished above us.

We ducked just in time. Then immediately we passed between the legs of another dinosaur. Miraculously, Professor P managed to miss all the dinosaurs and get us through unharmed.

"Sorry about that!" Professor P cried as we safely emerged the other side. "Is everyone all right?"

"Yes," Tara and I replied shakily.

"Is it over?" Brains moaned. "Can I look now?"

"Oh, Brains!" Floppy chided him. "Where's your sense of adventure! That was brilliant! In fact, I think with a few small adjustments we could go even faster!"

"Quite fast enough for me, I think, Floppy!" Professor P said as he adjusted the dial on the dashboard. "I'm going to take it much slower from now on!"

We continued across the plain, passing a group of palm trees. Then we went over a ridge, landing with a jolt on the other side. Professor P slowed the car and I looked around for the portal.

I could see the lake where we had been attacked by the allosaurs. There was no sign of them now. They were probably in hiding, scared by the noise from the car.

Suddenly, Tara shouted out, "Over there!"

Relieved, I saw the familiar yellow glow of the portal about two hundred metres away.

Professor P pressed a switch on the dashboard and the flames from the jet engine died away. The car slowed and came to a halt a short distance from the portal. He switched off the hover fan and there was silence at last.

My ears were ringing from the deafening roar of the jets. That was quite a ride! Professor P's invention had worked brilliantly and we had arrived safely at the portal.

Now, it was time to go home.

CHAPTER TWENTY TWO

Portal Problems

We got out of the car and went over to the portal. Professor P walked round the triangle and examined it. Floppy sat on his shoulder and peered at the portal through a large magnifying glass.

"Is everything all right, Professor P?" I asked.

"All in order," he replied confidently. "Floppy, I'll need your help to reprogram the portal's software. The quantum calculations are very complex."

"My pleasure," Floppy said proudly.

"Floppy and I will be a few minutes," Professor P told us. "Peter, Tara, you wait in the car with the dogs. Have the dino defences ready, just in case."

"Just in case!" Brains repeated nervously. "Where are you going, Professor P?"

"Floppy and I need to go through the portal," Professor P explained, "so we can get to the control box on the other side."

"Why?" Brains asked doubtfully.

"Because of my brilliant idea," Floppy said proudly. "We're going to reprogram the portal so it returns us to just after we left. Then Peter and Tara won't be late home for tea."

"Can I come too?" Brains asked hopefully.

"No, Brains, you stay here," Professor P replied firmly. "You need to look after Peter and Tara, and guard the portal. We won't be long."

Brains thought for a moment and then agreed, "All right," he said bravely.

"Just one thing," Professor P added as he walked towards the portal. "Don't come through while we're doing the reprogramming. Wait for us to come back or there's no telling where you might end up!"

"OK, Professor P," we choroused.

We watched Professor P and Floppy disappear into the yellow shimmering mist. Sleepy went over to the portal and lay down in front of it. She gazed into the mist, waiting patiently for her master to return.

"Mind your backs!" Brains called out.

I laughed as Brains marched back and forth in front of the portal, swinging his arms high.

Tara and I went and sat down in the back of the car. Sparky stayed outside, lying down in the shade.

"It's been quite an adventure, hasn't it, Tara?" I said.

"Yes," she replied wistfully.

"So much has happened and so quickly!" I added. "It was only a few days ago when Dotty's egg..."

I stopped. I should not have mentioned Dotty. Tara still seemed upset about leaving her.

"It's OK, Peter," Tara said calmly. "I know I've done the right thing for Dotty. She wouldn't be happy at home with me. This is her world and she needs to be with others of her kind. She'll be happy here."

"She will," I agreed comfortingly.

"And when we get home," Tara continued, "I'll ask my mum and dad if I can have another pet."

"A smaller one this time?" I joked.

"Definitely!" she replied, a smile returning to her face.

While we were waiting for Professor P to return, Tara took the dinosaur sketches out of her rucksack. I looked on in admiration as she shaded in the details. The drawings were brilliant. They would be perfect to go with our scelidosaurus fossil in the exhibition. Our fossil! It seemed a lifetime ago when we discovered it.

As Tara continued sketching, I gazed out at the view, trying to take in as much as I could before we went home. I watched a herd of diplodocus slowly move across the plain, gracefully waving their long tails. They shimmered in the haze as the sun beat down on the hot ground.

I looked up and saw a pterosaur flying overhead. How could such a huge creature ever get off the ground, I wondered? But yet, once in the air, it seemed to circle effortlessly, its huge wings catching the rising air currents like a glider.

It was wonderful to be here, surrounded by all these incredible creatures, ones I had only ever read about in books. I never imagined I would see them in real life. Now, I knew what the world of the dinosaurs was really like!

"This is better than copying from books!" Tara said as her hands flew over the page. "I've got all the sketches I need for our dinosaur guide, except for a scelidosaurus. It's a pity we never saw a real one."

"We'll have to come back for that!" I joked.

"Definitely!" she laughed.

Tara was putting the final touches to her drawings, when Brains marched over to the car.

"Where's Professor P?" he asked anxiously. "He's been gone for hours!"

"He's only been gone twenty minutes, Brains," I said, glancing at my watch.

"I think I'll just go through the portal and check…" Brains said, striding towards the portal.

"No!" Tara and I cried out.

"Professor P said we mustn't go through," I reminded him.

"Oh, yes, I forgot," Brains said sheepishly.

"I'm sure he'll be back soon," Tara reassured him.

Sure enough, a few moments later, there was a burst of yellow sparks from the portal. Sleepy jumped up and barked loudly.

Professor P and Floppy stepped out of the mist. They had returned safely!

"All done!" Professor P said happily as he came over to us.

"Can we go home now?" Brains asked eagerly.

"Not quite yet, Brains," Professor P replied. "We put a delay in the program so we'd have enough time to get back before the portal resets itself."

"It'll be ready in a jiffy," Floppy added.

We watched as the portal began to sparkle. Then suddenly, with a bright yellow flash, the triangle disappeared!

"It's gone!" Brains cried. "Professor P, the portal's gone!"

"Don't panic, Brains," Professor P said calmly. "It's all under control. It's meant to do that."

Moments later, with another flash, the portal reappeared!

"Excellent!" Professor P exclaimed. "Just as I expected. The portal has reset itself to the new time difference."

"We'll be back in time for tea!" Floppy said cheerfully.

"Good," Brains said relieved. "I've had enough excitement for today."

Professor P climbed back into the driver's seat and Sleepy jumped into the front seat of the car beside him.

"Come on, Sparky," I called, opening the door for him.

Sparky jumped onto my lap and wagged his tail happily.

Brains was about to get in the car, when Professor P stopped him.

"Can you lift the back of the car and push us through, please, Brains?" Professor P asked. "I don't want to risk using the jet engine near the portal."

"OK, Professor P," Brains replied confidently.

He went round to the back of the car and lifted it a short distance off the ground.

"Ouch!" he cried, dropping it suddenly. "It's hot!"

Floppy flew over to help.

"The bottom of the car is still hot from the jet engine," he explained to Brains. "Try lifting here at the top of the boot where the metal is cooler."

I felt the car rise up and move forward a few metres. Then Brains dropped it with a bump.

"I can't get a proper grip," he complained. "It's too heavy."

"Shall we get out, Professor P?" I suggested.

"Good idea," Professor P replied. "And could you take everything off the back seat, too. That should help to lighten the load."

Tara and I grabbed the rucksacks and got out of the car. Sparky jumped out and looked at me, puzzled. He had only just got into the car!

"That's better," Brains said, lifting the car higher this time.

"Wait a few minutes before you come through," Professor P said to us. "You must let the car get clear of the portal."

"OK, Professor P," we replied.

Professor P carefully steered the car towards the portal with Brains pushing hard. Sleepy stood on the front seat, her paws resting on the dashboard and her tongue hanging out. Floppy perched on Professor P's shoulder wearing his driving hat and goggles.

"See you on the other side!" Floppy called out as the car entered the portal.

Tara and I hung back and watched as the car disappeared into the yellow sparkling mist. I picked up Sparky and we waited a moment for the sparks to die down. Then Tara and I took one last look around at the amazing view and stepped into the portal together.

As before, it felt as though I was in a tunnel of sparkling yellow light. But now it felt as though I was treading on soft cotton wool. It was very difficult walking as my feet kept sinking into the strange mist.

Ahead, I could see the blurred outline of the car. Everything looked distorted, like a reflection from a fairground mirror.

We had almost reached the other side when a flash of light burst out from under my feet. I looked down and saw a large hole in the tunnel!

"Look out, Tara!" I cried, grabbing her arm and trying to pull her back.

But it was too late! Tara fell, taking Sparky and me with her. We plummeted down a funnel of swirling light, like spiders down a plughole. My heart was pounding as we spiralled downwards, out of control. I clutched onto Sparky tightly. I could feel him shaking with fear.

I shut my eyes, as the light grew brighter. Then I felt a strange sensation as my body seemed to dissolve into a sea of flashing rainbow coloured light.

A moment later, the light vanished and I felt solid again. Then I fell down onto hard wet ground.

I lay on the cold ground, my head spinning and stomach churning. I could hear the sound of waves breaking and smell salty air. I felt dizzy and was shivering with cold. As I lay there motionless, I felt a warm tongue lick my face.

"Oh, Sparky!" I spluttered as I sat up. "I can see you're OK!"

When my head stopped spinning, I tried to stand up but almost lost my balance. My legs felt very wobbly, as though I had just stepped off a fast fairground ride.

When I felt more steady, I looked around. I was on a pebbly beach not far from some cliffs. A thick mist covered the sea and hid the top of the cliffs. Tara was sitting on the pebbles a few metres away, rubbing her knee.

"Are you all right, Tara?" I asked as I went over to her.

"I grazed my knee," she replied shakily, getting to her feet. "But I'm OK."

"That was weird!" I said.

"I know," Tara replied. "I remember stepping into the mist. After that, it's like a dream. I can't remember…"

She broke off, a look of concentration on her face. "No it's gone," she added.

I felt the same. Already the journey through the portal was fading fast. It seemed such a long time ago.

"I thought we would come back to the island," I said, confused.

"Me too," Tara said, equally puzzled.

"And where is Professor P?" I said, suddenly. "He came through first so he should be here by now."

We looked around, puzzled. I peered into the mist, straining to see any signs of Professor P or the car. But the fog was so thick, I could not see anything clearly.

I shivered in the cold wind, not sure what to do. Should we wait here or go home? And which way was home?

"Sparky! Home!" I said firmly.

"Woof!" he barked and ran along the beach.

Tara and I followed, hoping Sparky knew where he was going. We stumbled along the pebbly beach until finally I realised we were on the East beach, not far from the car park.

"Maybe Professor P is waiting for us in the car park," I said hopefully.

Tara and I bounded up the steps and waited for Sparky at the top. As we waited, the mist began to clear and I looked out to sea. I saw a few fishing boats close to the shore and...

I gasped in astonishment!

"Tara, look!" I cried in disbelief. "The island! It's gone!"

CHAPTER TWENTY THREE

The Dinosaur Shop

I stared out to sea, unable to believe my eyes. The island had completely disappeared!

Tara turned to me, astonished.

"What…how…?" she spluttered.

"Something's wrong, Tara," I said anxiously. "I don't think we can be home!"

"Where are we then?" she asked, confused.

"I don't know," I replied, "but I think we'd better find out."

I put Sparky on the lead and we set off. As we walked through the car park, I looked around for Professor P's car. But there was no sign of it. By the ticket machine, I noticed a rusty old van. It looked like the one that had been parked there all week but it was green and not red. I stared at it, puzzled.

As we made our way up the hill, I heard a sharp cry overhead. I looked up and saw a dark shape disappear behind the trees. Sparky growled in warning. I shivered uneasily.

"What was that?" Tara asked apprehensively.

"I'm not sure," I replied, "but it was too big to be a seagull."

I felt nervous as we walked towards the village, unsure what we would find there. When we arrived, Sparky tugged at the lead and we followed him onto the green. Everything looked the same but Sparky sniffed the ground suspiciously. The hair on his back stood up; he seemed to sense something was wrong.

We continued walking across the green. Suddenly, Tara burst out, "Look, Peter! Mary's shop!"

I glanced across the village square. The fossil shop was still there but something was different…

"The name!" she exclaimed.

Tara was right! The name had changed. The large silver sign hanging above the window now read, *The Dinosaur Shop*.

We ran over to have a closer look. In the window was a large poster that read, "*Order your Dinosaurs here! All types available – from small household pets to large guard–dinosaurs.*"

"Dinosaur pets?" I cried in astonishment.

"It must be a joke!" Tara said as she pushed open the door.

We went inside and cautiously glanced around. Mary was behind the counter, serving a woman. She looked up when we came in and smiled.

"Morning, Peter, Tara," she greeted us cheerfully. "I'll be with you shortly."

As Mary went back to serving her customer, I looked around the shop. At first glance, it seemed the same as before. By the window were the same neat shelves of ammonites and belemnites fossils. Purple amethyst crystals sparkled in the display cabinet by the door. The huge ichthyosaurs fossil still hung impressively above the counter. Pinned to the wall was the newspaper article about the recent landslide.

Suddenly, Tara gasped and pointed to the far wall. We dashed over and looked in astonishment at the displays. Here was everything you could possibly need for a dinosaur pet! Hanging from the wall, were brightly coloured collars and leads. I read a note attached to a red saddle, *children's saddle suitable for riding Ornithomimus and Gallimimus*.

"Dinosaur riding!" Tara exclaimed. "But how…?

"I've no idea!" I replied, equally bewildered.

Above the display was a large sign which read, *Always buy your dinosaur eggs from an approved dealer! You must have a licence to own guard-dinosaurs larger than 1.5 metres.*

"Guard-dinosaurs!" I cried in disbelief.

How could it be? What had happened to Mary's shop?

We continued looking at the rest of the display. On a shelf next to the collars, were scratching pads, wire brushes and pairs of pliers. I picked up the pliers and read the label, *To keep those sharp claws in trim!*

In the corner, a pile of dried food boxes was stacked into a pyramid. Sparky ran over and sniffed at the boxes eagerly. I picked up one of the boxes and read the label. *DinoCrunch. Formulated for the fussy eater!*

One of the shelves was devoted to health care and was filled with coloured bottles. A poster above the shelf read, *Dinosaurs need calcium for healthy skin and teeth.*

Eventually, Mary's customer left the shop and she came over to us.

"Sorry to keep you waiting," Mary apologised, "I sold that lady a pet compsognathus for her daughter last week and I'm afraid it's been behaving rather badly!"

Before we had a chance to say anything, Mary continued, "Oh, I expect you've come about your dinosaur guide? I'll just go and get it."

As Mary went over to the counter, I looked at Tara, bewildered.

"Dinosaur guide!" I exclaimed.

Mary returned with the sheets of paper. I read the contents in astonishment, *Allosaurus, Apatosaurus, Brachiosaurus...* Tara and I leafed through the pages in astonishment. This was the dinosaur guide we had been working on – but now it was completely finished!

"It's an excellent booklet to go with your exhibition," Mary said enthusiastically. "I really like your Fun Facts! I think you'll sell plenty..."

Unable to contain myself any longer, I burst out, "Mary, where did all this dinosaur stuff come from?"

"Where did it come from?" Mary repeated, looking at us puzzled. "I don't understand..."

"But the dinosaurs died out!" Tara exclaimed.

"Millions of years ago..." I added.

"Sixty five million year ago, to be precise," Mary said, "at the end of the cretaceous period."

"But if dinosaurs are extinct..." I began.

"Were extinct," Mary corrected.

"Who brought them back to life?" I asked.

"The scientists!" Mary exclaimed. "Everyone knows that!"

Mary looked at us concerned, "Are you two feeling all right?" she asked.

I did not know what to say. I felt totally confused!

"But how?" Tara asked.

"Oh, so that's what you mean!" Mary said, smiling. "You're doing a science project at school on *how* they brought the dinosaurs back to life?"

Tara and I glanced at each other, not sure how to reply.

"I'm afraid I don't know exactly how they did it," Mary continued, happily. "It had something to do with chicken's eggs…"

"Chicken's eggs?" we repeated.

"Yes," Mary replied. "Chickens share a common ancestor with the dinosaurs. So scientists used genetic engineering to turn a chicken back into a dinosaur."

"Have all the dinosaurs come back to life?" I asked in astonishment.

"Oh, no!" Mary exclaimed. "Only a few species. But scientists are coming up with new breeds all the time. I've got a magazine with an article about it, if you're interested in the details."

"Thanks," I replied, still feeling very confused.

Mary went over to the counter, picked up the magazine and gave it to us.

"Oh, before I forget, Tara," Mary added, "your order of Baby DinoCrunch has arrived."

"DinoCrunch?" Tara repeated blankly.

"The one you ordered last week," Mary continued, reaching under the counter.

She brought out a large box. On the cover was a picture of a diplodocus.

"This large size box should last you a few weeks," Mary added, "and it's specially formulated for miniature diplodocus…"

"Miniature diplodocus?" Tara interrupted.

"Yes," Mary replied. "You said Dotty was a fussy eater…"

"Dotty!" Tara exclaimed.

"Are you all right, Tara?" Mary asked, looking worried. "Is something the matter?"

Tara did not reply. She just stared at Mary, totally bewildered.

"Mary, did you say Dotty?" I asked tentatively.

"Yes," Mary replied. "Tara's pet…"

"I've got to go!" Tara cried, rushing over to the door.

"Don't forget your…" Mary called after her.

But Tara had already left. I picked up the box of DinoCrunch and called to Sparky.

"Thanks, Mary," I said dashing to the door.

Sparky and I ran after Tara. She sprinted up the hill so fast we could barely keep pace with her. When we finally caught up with her, she was outside her house, fumbling with the key in the lock.

She opened the front door and burst inside. Sparky and I followed her into the hallway.

"Dotty! Dotty!" Tara panted.

We went into the living room but there was no sign of Dotty. Tara rushed into the kitchen. On the table was a note, which read, *Tara, gone shopping with Rosie, back about 1.00pm, help yourself to ammonite bites if you're hungry, love Mum.*

"Woof! Woof!" Sparky barked.

He was in the corner of the room, wagging his tail excitedly. He had found a large wooden cage with a glass front. Tara and I went over to have a look. I bent down and saw a bowl of water and some leaves on the bottom of the cage. But no Dotty!

We raced upstairs and went into Tara's bedroom.

"Dotty!" Tara called out again.

Still there was no reply. Tara quickly searched the room for any sign of the dinosaur.

"Oh, where can she be?" Tara cried in frustration.

"Maybe she's in Rosie's room?" I suggested.

Tara ran next door into Rosie's bedroom.

"Dotty!" she called out impatiently.

"Eeek! Eeek," came a familiar cry.

A little creature popped its head out from under a pile of dinosaur toys in the middle of the floor. It looked up at Tara, wide-eyed. It was Dotty!

Tara picked up Dotty and held her tightly.

"Dotty," she cried, her eyes filling with tears. "It is you! I thought I'd never see you again!"

Tara sat down on the floor and Dotty climbed onto her lap. As I watched the baby dinosaur nuzzle Tara affectionately, my mind was filled with questions. Why was Dotty here? Why had Mary's shop changed? Where had the island gone? And what had happened to Professor P?

I felt very confused. We had obviously returned home but not to the same home we had left.

"Tara, we need to find Professor P," I said urgently.

Tara looked up at me, her face beaming with happiness. She was so pleased to have Dotty back.

"We need to find out what's going on," I insisted.

"OK," she nodded, seeing my concern.

Tara put Dotty down on the floor and stood up.

"I'll be back soon, Dotty," she said kindly.

"Eeek! Eeek!" Dotty cried and waddled happily back to the pile of dinosaur toys.

"It doesn't make sense!" I said as we walked downstairs. "Everything's the same, but different…"

"And I've got Dotty back!" Tara cried, delighted.

I had never seen Tara so happy. I was really pleased for her but I needed to know what had caused things to change. How had we got here? Was this really our home?

"I'm sure Professor P will know what's going on, Peter," Tara said reassuringly.

I put Sparky on the lead and we left the house. As we walked up the main road, Sparky ran ahead, tugging at the lead. He stopped by a gate leading to a farmer's field and barked suspiciously.

"What is it, Sparky?" I asked, looking over the gate.

I gasped in amazement at the huge animals grazing in the field. They had small heads, short necks, long tails and were covered in hard bumpy armour.

"Look, Peter!" Tara cried, pointing to a sign on the gate. It read, *Keep Out! Scelidosaurs Grazing!*

"Scelidosaurs!" I exclaimed.

"Real ones!" Tara added. "Our fossil has come alive!"

We watched in astonishment as the huge dinosaurs lumbered about the field, swinging their long armoured tails. One of them turned to look at us, then lowered its head and continued grazing.

Sparky tugged on the lead again, eager to move on. We left the field of scelidosaurus and hurried up the hill to Farmyard Lane. As we ran along the path leading to Professor P house, I wondered what we would find.

Would Professor P even be there?

CHAPTER TWENTY FOUR

Honeydew Cottage

When we reached the gate outside Professor P's house, I noticed a sign that read, *Welcome to Honeydew Cottage*. But it used to be called Honeysuckle Cottage!

I glanced up at the house, looking to see if there were any other differences. The ivy had been neatly cut back and the window frames were gleaming white. They looked as though they had just been painted. Apart from that the house looked the same as before.

"Do you think this is still Professor P house, Tara?" I asked as I pushed open the gate.

"We'll soon find out," she replied as we walked down the gravel path.

As we stepped into the porch, a voice spoke to us.

"Ah, Peter, Tara and Sparky! Welcome!" the door greeted us in a calm and courteous manner.

I breathed a sigh of relief. This was Professor P's house all right!

"Is Professor P in?" I asked.

"Yes, he's in the back garden," the door replied. "Would you use the side passage, please? We've just had the carpets cleaned. Thank you."

"What a nice door!" Tara said as we went over to the side gate.

I opened the gate and we walked along the gravel path around the side of the cottage. As we reached the corner of the house, I heard Professor P shout, "Look out, Brains!" followed by a loud crash.

"Quick!" I cried. "Sounds like there's been an accident!"

Sparky barked and ran ahead. We dashed into the back garden and I gasped in astonishment at what I saw!

In the middle of the lawn was a huge metal scaffolding. Professor P was hanging precariously from the top, his legs swinging about wildly. Floppy was circling above him as a purple pterodactyl, flapping his wings frantically.

Sparky ran over to join Sleepy, who was resting her paws on the scaffolding. She was looking up at Professor P and barking anxiously. Brains was lying in front of the scaffolding, flat on his back with a long ladder pinning him to the ground. His arms and legs were flailing about. He looked like an upturned beetle!

"Peter, Tara!" Floppy cried, as he flew down to us. "Thank goodness you're here! You've arrived just in time! Quick, get the ladder off Brains!"

We ran over to Brains, lifted the heavy ladder off him and helped him to his feet. Then, with Brains' help, we picked up the ladder and rested it against the scaffolding. We held the base securely so Professor P could climb down.

As Professor P came down the ladder, I noticed that he had long hair tied up in a ponytail! Tara saw it and giggled.

"Peter, Tara, you saved the day!" Professor P said as he stepped onto the lawn. "Thank you!"

"That's all right," we chorused.

"Are you all right Brains?" Professor P asked, noticing the robot swaying unsteadily from side to side.

"Indubitably," Brains replied.

I looked at Tara in surprise. I had never heard Brains use such a big word!

"But the ground keeps moving, Professor P!" Brains added lamely.

I chuckled. Brains was the same as usual!

"We'll take a break now and finish work later," Professor P said kindly.

"Good," Brains said, exhausted.

"Oh, I expect you're wondering what this is going to be," Professor P said, pointing towards the scaffolding.

I noticed a pile of shiny yellow tubes lying on the ground by the scaffolding. Professor P was in the middle of building a portal!

"My latest invention is…"

Before he could finish, Floppy raised a trumpet to his lips and blew a loud fanfare.

"A work of genius!" Floppy announced. "It's an Inter Dimensional…"

"Portal," Tara and I burst out.

Floppy stared at us in surprise.

"You know!" he cried, indignantly. "But you can't… Professor P, they can't know! It's our secret!"

Professor P looked at us intently. "How do you know about the portal?" he asked curiously.

"We've already been through it," I replied.

"You've already been through the portal?" Professor P repeated in astonishment. "But that's impossible!"

"No, really, we have," I insisted.

"Yesterday, on the island…" Tara began.

"Island?" Floppy squawked. "What island?"

"The one in the bay…" Tara continued.

"But it's not there any more," I interrupted.

"I'm lost," Floppy said, shaking his head slowly.

"We went through the portal to get some food for Dotty," Tara explained, "from the Jurassic…"

"You've been to the Jurassic!" Professor P cried in disbelief.

"Yes, but when we came back, things were different…" I began.

"There are dinosaurs here!" Tara added. "Real dinosaurs!"

"Well, of course there are!" Floppy exclaimed.

"But they weren't when we left," I said.

"Fascinating!" Professor P said, his eyes sparkling with delight. "You must tell me everything that's happened! Let's go into the kitchen and have a drink."

We all went through the back door into the kitchen. I chuckled when I saw the state of the room – it was even messier than ever! Boxes full of toasters and kettles littered the floor. The work surfaces were piled high with electronic components, circuit boards and bundles of wires.

As I looked around, I noticed a large cardboard box balancing precariously on the top of the fridge. Scribbled on the box in black marker pen were the words, *Dazzling Dinosaur Devices*.

Brains walked unsteadily to the table and sat down abruptly. He held his head, as if it might fall off!

"Tara, look!" I said, pointing at the table.

Lying on the table were two small dinosaurs! They were tiny stegosaurs with bright orange plates on their back.

"Oh, they're cute!" Tara exclaimed.

Professor P gently picked them up and put them in their basket.

"What are their names, Professor P?" Tara asked, stroking their heads.

"The fatter one is called Cuddle-osaurus and the other is called Claw-osaurus," Professor P replied.

"Cuddles and Claws for short," Floppy added.

Professor P put some dried dog food in a bowl for Sleepy and Sparky. Then he put two glasses of orange juice and a plate of biscuits on the table for us.

Professor P took a kettle out of one of the boxes on the floor and filled it with water. It was round and orange with a large smiling face painted on it.

"Anyone for a joke?" the kettle burst out as Professor P switched it on. "You'll love this one. I made it up myself! How do you get six dinosaurs into a car?"

Tara looked at me and giggled.

"Two in the front, two in the back and two in the boot!" the kettle burst out before we had a chance to answer.

As Professor P waited for the kettle to boil, it chuckled away to itself, "How do I do it?...I'm so funny!...I even amaze myself!"

The water started to boil but the kettle did not switch itself off. As Professor P reached for the switch a flash of sparks flew from the kettle.

"Oops," the kettle said. "I think I've blown a fuse!"

Tara and I burst out laughing. Professor P's talking inventions were just as silly as ever!

Professor P made himself a cup of tea and sat down at the table with us.

"Now, Peter, Tara," he said eagerly. "Why don't you tell me everything? Start from the beginning."

"I got an egg for Easter," Tara began. "It hatched and..."

"A chocolate egg hatched?" Brains interrupted. "I didn't know they could do that!"

"It wasn't a chocolate egg," Tara chuckled. "It was a real one. And out came Dotty."

"What's a Dotty?" Brains said confused.

"She's a diplodocus," Tara replied. "That's a type of dinosaur..."

"But you said there weren't any dinosaurs..." Brains interrupted again.

"There weren't," Tara replied. "But Floppy got one for me. From the IGW."

"The IG what?" Brains repeated, confused.

"The Intergalactic Web," I explained. "It's like the World Wide Web but with aliens..."

"Aliens! You're making this up!" Brains exclaimed. "Professor P, they're pulling your leg!"

"No, it's true," Tara protested.

"You found an important formula on the IGW, Professor P," I added. "You used it to make the portal work."

"Now that is very interesting," Professor P said looking at Floppy knowingly, "we shall have to investigate the IGW!"

"Definitely," Floppy agreed, nodding excitedly.

"I'm still confused about these aliens," Brains said, shaking his head.

"I'll explain later," Professor P said kindly. "Let's allow Peter and Tara to finish their story, first, Brains."

"Dotty wouldn't eat anything," Tara continued. "So we went through the portal to get some food for her."

"We went back to the Jurassic!" I said excitedly. "It was amazing!"

"And we were attacked by a huge allosaurs!" Tara added.

"But your dino defences saved us, Professor P," I explained happily, "with help from Brains!"

"Me!" Brains said, surprised.

"Yes, you were brilliant, Brains," I said encouragingly.

"Thanks," Brains said proudly.

"Then we got to the forest and found some food for Dotty," Tara continued. "And we were having so much fun we decided to camp the night!"

"Using your Adventure Inventions, Professor P," I added excitedly.

"But when we got back to the car in the morning, it was squashed," Tara said. "A dinosaur had knocked a tree onto it."

"So you turned the car into a hoverjet, Professor P!" I said. "It went like a bomb! We reached the portal in no time!"

"But when we came back through the portal," Tara added, "things were different."

"The island was gone" I said, "and the fossil shop is different…"

"And Dotty's back home again!" Tara burst out happily.

"Do you know what's going on Professor P?" I asked.

Professor P sat quietly and stroked his beard thoughtfully. We waited patiently for him to reply

"I know exactly what has happened," he replied finally. "I'm just trying to work out how best to explain it."

"It's the butterfly effect, isn't it Professor P," Floppy said, turning into a bright purple butterfly and flapping his wings, causing a tornado to appear around him.

"Yes, exactly, Floppy," Professor P nodded. "The butterfly effect! A tiny change can have a huge effect."

I looked at Tara puzzled.

"When you went back in time," Professor P continued, "you changed it very slightly by being there. Over the years, that has caused a big effect on the present. That's why the portal brought you here…"

"But what happened to the world Peter and Tara left," Brains interrupted. "Where did it go? And what happened to the other Brains? Is he all right?"

"There's no need to worry, Brains," Floppy reassured him. "Everything is fine! The world that Peter and Tara left no longer exists. It changed into this one and everything in it changed too. The other Brains changed into you…"

"That's OK, then," Brains said, relieved.

"So this is Peter and Tara's home, now!" Professor P announced.

"And I think you'll find it's a lot more fun here!" Floppy said excitedly.

"If you like dinosaurs, that is!" Professor P said with a twinkle in his eye.

Tara looked at me, delighted. Her face beamed with excitement. I could see what she was thinking. She had Dotty back and we would have the adventure of a lifetime, living in the world of the dinosaurs!

Fantastic!

THE END?

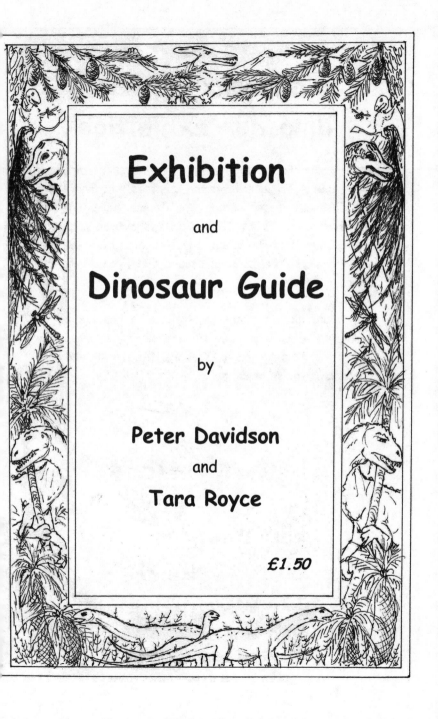

Exhibition

and

Dinosaur Guide

by

Peter Davidson

and

Tara Royce

£1.50

Welcome to our dinosaur exhibition

We really hope you enjoy visiting our dinosaur exhibition. The exhibition centres around the scelidosaurus fossil which we found here on the Jurassic Coast. This little guide will show you what the scelidosaurs was like when it was alive and will tell you about some of the other dinosaurs that lived during the Jurassic Period.

We would like to thank everyone who has helped us make the exhibition and this fossil guide, especially Mary for helping us to prepare the fossil and for allowing us to use her shop.

Best wishes,

Peter & Tara

Contents

Introduction to Dinosaurs

What is a dinosaur?

A dinosaur is a type of animal with scaly skin, called a reptile. The smallest dinosaurs, like compsognathus, were about the size of a chicken and the largest, like diplodocus were over 30 metres long.

When did they live?

Dinosaurs first appeared about 230 million years ago during the Triassic Period. They died out 65 millions years ago at the end of the Cretaceous Period.

Why did they die out?

A huge asteroid (larger than the Isle of Wight) smashed into the earth 65 million years ago. Scientists believe it would have sent up huge clouds of dust and smoke, blocking out sunlight and killing the plants. Without food the dinosaurs would soon have died out.

How many types of dinosaur are there?

About 1,000 species of dinosaur have been discovered so far but more are being found all the time.

DINOSAUR GUIDE

What are the different types of dinosaur?

Dinosaurs are grouped together into families with similar characteristics called suborders. Here are some of the common Jurassic suborders

Suborder	Description	Example dinosaur
Ornithopods (Bird footed)	Ornithopods commonly walked on two legs. They had beaks and no body armor.	Dryosaurus
Sauropods (Lizard footed)	Sauropods walked on four legs. They were huge plant eaters with long necks and small heads. They lived at least 100 years.	Brachiosaurus
Theropods (Beast footed)	Theropods walked on two legs. They were fast moving meat eaters with sharp teeth and claws.	Megalosaurus
Thyreophorans (Shield bearers)	Thyreophorans were heavily armored plant eating dinosaurs.	Stegosaurus

Allosaurus

Powerful Predator

Allosaurus was one of the largest and most powerful meat-eating dinosaurs of the Jurassic Period. It walked on two powerful legs built for speed; they had strong muscles and heavy bones.

Although its arms were short, each finger on its three-fingered hands was armed with a sharp claw 15 cm long. Its enormously powerful jaws were filled with sabre-like serrated teeth. It may have hunted in packs to ambush the very large sauropods like Diplodocus.

6

Allosaurus

FACT FILE	
NAME	**Pronounced**: AL-oh-SAWR-us **Meaning**: Different lizard
SIZE	 **Length**: Up to 12 m long **Height**: Up to 3 m tall at hips **Weight**: Up to 5 tonnes in weight
TYPE	Theropod
DIET	Meat eater
PERIOD	Late Jurassic, about 155-145 million years ago

Did you know?

The name allosaurus means *different lizard* because of its unusual backbone, which is lighter than those of other dinosaurs.

Apatosaurus

Heavyweight Hulk

Apatosaurus was one of the largest land animals that ever existed, weighing more than four elephants! Its enormous size helped protect it from predators, which could not reach its head or neck.

It ate only leaves and plants, using its long neck to reach deep into the forest. Its tiny head had blunt pencil-like teeth, arranged like a garden rake and used for stripping leaves. It did not chew its food; instead, it swallowed stones to help grind up its food

Apatosaurus

FACT FILE	
NAME	**Pronounced**: a-PAT-o-SAWR-us **Meaning**: Deceptive lizard
SIZE	 **Length**: Up to 27 m long **Height**: Up to 5 m tall at hips **Weight**: Up to 35 tonnes in weight
TYPE	Sauropod
DIET	Plant eater
PERIOD	Late Jurassic, about 157-146 million years ago

Did you know?
Apatosaurus' nostrils were located on the top of its head. No one knows why!

Brachiosaurus

Tremendously Tall

Brachiosaurus was one of the tallest animals that ever existed. It had a very small head with 52 teeth. It spent almost all of its waking hours feeding – needing to eat about 200kg of food each day!

Brachiosaurus was so tall it needed to have a very powerful heart to pump blood up the long neck to its head and brain. Its blood pressure was probably four times as high as ours.

Brachiosaurus

FACT FILE	
NAME	**Pronounced**: BRAK-e-o-SAWR-us **Meaning**: Arm lizard
SIZE	 **Length**: Up to 25 m long **Height**: Up to 7 m tall (hips), 15 m (head) **Weight**: Up to 50 tonnes in weight
TYPE	Sauropod
DIET	Plant eater
PERIOD	Late Jurassic, about 156-145 million years ago

Did you know?

Unlike most other dinosaurs, the front legs of Brachiosaurus were longer than the hind legs – hence its name, *arm lizard*.

Compsognathus

Small and Smart

Compsognathus was one of the smallest known dinosaurs, about the size of a chicken. It walked on two long, thin legs; it was a fast, agile dinosaur with a long flexible tail, which helped it keep its balance.

Compsognathus had a small, pointed head filled with small, sharp curved teeth. It ate small animals, including insects and lizards.

Compsognathus

FACT FILE	
NAME	**Pronounced**: KOMP-sog-NAH-thus **Meaning**: Elegant or pretty jaw
SIZE	 **Length**: Up to 1 m long **Height**: Up to 25cm tall at hips **Weight**: Up to 3 kg in weight
TYPE	Theropod
DIET	Meat eater
PERIOD	Late Jurassic, about 155-145 million years ago

Did you know?

A compsognathus fossil found in the 1850s was the first complete dinosaur fossil to be discovered. But scientists at the time did not realise it was a dinosaur – they thought it was too small!

13

Diplodocus

Terrible Tail

Diplodocus was one of the longest land animals ever to have lived. Its tail was 14 metres long with up to 80 backbones in it. If attacked, it used the tail as a whip, cracking it through the air to frighten predators away.

Underneath its backbone were extra bones running both forwards and backwards in the shape of an anvil. This 'double beam' gives the diplodocus its name.

Diplodocus

FACT FILE	
NAME	**Pronounced**: di-PLOD-o-kus **Meaning**: Double beamed
SIZE	 **Length**: Up to 30 m long **Height**: Up to 5 m tall at hips **Weight**: Up to 20 tonnes in weight
TYPE	Sauropod
DIET	Plant eater
PERIOD	Late Jurassic, about 155-145 million years ago

Did you know?

When diplodocus cracked its tail, the tip could reach speeds up to a thousand miles an hour! Oddly enough, it could not lift its head much higher than its shoulders.

15

Dryosaurus

Rapid Runner

Dryosaurus was a fast, agile, two-legged dinosaur with large eyes and long, thin legs. Running was its main defence against predators.

Dryosaurus had a horny beak, a toothless upper front jaw, and self-sharpening cheek teeth, which it used to eat leaves in the forest. It carefully laid its eggs in nests and cared for its young.

Dryosaurus

FACT FILE	
NAME	**Pronounced**: dry-oh-SAWR-us **Meaning**: Oak lizard
SIZE	 **Length**: Up to 4 m long **Height**: Up to 1.5 m tall at hips **Weight**: Up to 90 kg in weight
TYPE	Ornithopod
DIET	Plant eater
PERIOD	Late Jurassic, about 156-145 million years ago

Did you know?

Scientists believe dryosaurus may have stored food in its cheeks. Dryosaurus means *oak lizard*, due to the oak like shape of its cheek teeth.

Megalosaurus

Mighty Meat-eater

Megalosaurus was one of the fiercest meat-eating dinosaurs of the mid-Jurassic. It walked on two powerful legs, had a strong, short neck, and a large head with sharp, serrated teeth. It could kill even large sauropods, although it often preferred to scavenge for its food.

A megalosaurus thighbone found in Oxfordshire in 1676 was the first recorded dinosaur fossil ever to be found. Many years later, in 1824, it was given its scientific name, from the Greek megalo - meaning giant and saurus - meaning lizard.

Megalosaurus

FACT FILE	
NAME	**Pronounced**: MEG-ah-loh-SAWR-us **Meaning**: Great lizard
SIZE	 **Length**: Up to 10 m long **Height**: Up to 3 m tall at hips **Weight**: Up to 1 tonnes in weight
TYPE	Theropod
DIET	Meat eater
PERIOD	Late Jurassic, about 181-169 million years ago

Did you know?

Although megalosaurus was the first dinosaur to be found, a complete fossil has yet to be discovered!

Ornitholestes

Egg Eater

Ornitholestes was a fast and agile dinosaur that walked on two legs. It had long grasping hands, vicious claws and its mouth was filled with many small, sharp teeth. It ate eggs and small animals such as lizards and mammals living in the forest. It was perfectly designed for hunting in the undergrowth.

Its long tail was used for balance and agility, allowing it to change directions quickly as it chased prey.

Ornitholestes

FACT FILE	
NAME	**Pronounced**: OR-nith-oh-LEZ-teez **Meaning**: Bird robber
SIZE	 **Length**: Up to 2 m long **Height**: Up to 0.5 m tall at hips **Weight**: Up to 12 kg in weight
TYPE	Theropod
DIET	Meat eater
PERIOD	Late Jurassic, about 156-145 million years ago

Did you know?

Only one (almost complete) fossil of ornitholestes has ever been found!

Scelidosaurus

Peaceful Plant-eater

Scelidosaurus was a heavily armoured, plant-eating dinosaur with a small head, short neck, leaf-shaped teeth and a long, stiff tail. It had a small bony beak, which it used to rip off vegetation such as cycads.

Scelidosaurus walked on four legs but was able to rear up on its hind legs to reach tree branches.

Scelidosaurus

FACT FILE	
NAME	**Pronounced**: SKEL-eye-doh-SAWR-us **Meaning**: Limb lizard
SIZE	 **Length**: Up to 4 m long **Height**: Up to 1 m tall at hips **Weight**: Up to 250 kg in weight
TYPE	Thyreophoran
DIET	Plant eater
PERIOD	Early Jurassic, about 208-194 million years ago

Did you know?

Scelidosaurus was the first complete dinosaur ever found.

Stegosaurus

Peculiar Plates

Stegosaurus was a heavily armoured plant-eating dinosaur, which walked on four legs. It had 17 bony plates running along on its back in two rows. Its name means roof lizard and comes from the fact that these bony plates look like roof tiles.

Stegosaurus also had spikes at the end of its tail to protect it. They are called thagomizers!

Stegosaurus

FACT FILE	
NAME	**Pronounced**: STEG-o-SAWR-us **Meaning**: Roof or plated lizard
SIZE	 **Length**: Up to 9 m long **Height**: Up to 2.75 m tall at hips **Weight**: Up to 3 tonnes in weight
TYPE	Thyreophoran
DIET	Plant eater
PERIOD	Late Jurassic, about 156-140 million years ago

Did you know?

Stegosaurus had a very tiny brain
- it was only the size of a walnut!

Professor P's website

Visit **www.professorp.co.uk** for -

Deleted scenes

So many great scenes wouldn't fit into the book! But don't worry – they're all free on the website. Here are some of my favourites -

Tara's party

It's Christmas time and everyone is invited to Tara house for a party. Fun ensues when Professor P tries to fix Tara's broken computer. And it's mayhem when Brains turns up uninvited!

Snow Storm

There's a snow storm on the Jurassic Coast. It's just the excuse Professor P needs to try out his amazing jet skis!

Professor P's deleted invention

Discover some of Professor P's fantastic inventions that never made it into the book. There his self-inflating Christmas tree, the robot moles in charge of tunnelling out his basement and my favourite, his Clever Compass!

Fun facts

Are you interested in science, fossils and dinosaurs?
Look on the website to find out more –

Fossils

Learn about how to find and prepare fossils. Discover
the best places to find fossils.

Dinosaurs

Will scientists ever be able to bring the dinosaurs back
to life?

Time travel

Can you go back in time and change the past?

Games

Try out some exciting new games –

Fossil and dinosaur games

Can you work out how to fit fossil bones together to
make up a completed dinosaur?

Professor P trivial quiz

How well do you know Professor P?

Also by P.J. Davidson –

Professor P
and the
Jurassic Coast

An Amazing Adventure in Time

Peter and Tara have just moved to the Jurassic
Coast. While searching for fossils on the beach
they hear a mysterious explosion from beyond
the cliffs. This is the start of a fantastic
adventure with Professor P - one that will
change their world forever! Professor P and the
Jurassic Coast is an exciting story about the
time when dinosaurs ruled the Earth.

**Includes a 16 page illustrated fossil guide
full of fun and interesting facts.**

About Positive Books

We are an independent publisher specialising in positive, non-violent and educational books. Our books are manufactured by FSC accredited printers.

These books are available at your local bookstore and online:

Professor P and the Jurassic Coast   by P.J. Davidson   £7.99
Professor P and the Jurassic Island   by P.J. Davidson   £6.99

They can also be ordered directly from us. Please send cheque/postal order (Sterling only) made payable to Positive Books Limited to:

Positive Books Limited
66 High Street
Glastonbury
Somerset BA6 9DZ

Postage is free in the UK. Please add £2.00 per book for overseas. Please allow 28 days for delivery.

For availability of signed and dedicated copies please check our website:
www.positive-books.co.uk

Prices and availability are subject to change without notice.
When placing your order, please mention if you do not wish to receive further information.